Have you signed up for my newsletter yet?

I send out exclusive sneak peeks of all my new releases and giveaways plus a periodic newsletter where we can get to know each other. I'd love to have you. And, as a special thank you for being a part of my News Friends, I will send you a link to download a FREE eBook copy of my novella, *Of Walls*. You can sign up here:

http://eepurl.com/cfqP5H

Also by Sara L. Foust

ROMANTIC SUSPENSE:

LOVE, HOPE AND FAITH SERIES–

SMOKY MOUNTAIN SUSPENSE SERIES–

Women's fiction:

THE DROWNING OF CORINNE PORTER

Smoky Mountain Suspense Book Three

Sara L. Foust

The Drowning of Corinne Porter, Smoky Mountain Suspense Book Three

©2021 Sara L. Foust

Published by Silver Lining Literary Services, LLC
106 Offutt Rd.
Clinton, TN 37716
www.saralfoust.com

Printed in the United States of America

The persons and events portrayed in this work of fiction are the creations of the author, and any resemblance to persons living or dead is purely coincidental.

ISBN: 978-1-7329047-3-6

Scripture quoted is from the King James Version of the Bible, which is in public domain.
©2021 Cover Design by Sara L. Foust

For Mayci

My amazing, funny, big-hearted third born. You make me laugh every single day. Be strong and courageous, but most importantly always be you, my little cuddle bug.

And we know that all things work together for good to them that love God, to them who are called according to *his* purpose.

Romans 8:28 KJV

Chapter One

Helene's knees were killing her. When did she get so old? Thirty-eight was far too young to be falling apart. She snickered. Tell that to her psychologist, her primary physician, her friends, her everyone that was worried about her lately.

She stepped off the last little rock, landing her well-worn hiking boots solidly in a muddy puddle creek-side. Thank heavens for the magical waterproofing gods who made these things. Her socks still remained dry.

Helene climbed over boulders at the base of Abram's Falls until she made it close enough to feel the massive spray on her summer-heated face. She closed her eyes, lifted her arms to the sky, and took a deep, cleansing breath, letting it out slowly. Hiking always cleared her head of the pesky voices. Of the self-doubt. Of the tendency to lose herself within.

Weekdays were better for hiking. Fewer other hikers to spoil the solitude. A bird broke into song overhead, and Helene allowed her eyes to open slowly. Standing atop a huge rock, she let her gaze fall into the strong current before her.

An involuntary scream erupted from her, bouncing off the tall waterfall and fading into the empty forest.

Was this another hallucination, or was a body truly lying prostrate at the bottom of this deep natural pool?

Three hours and four minutes later, Helene waited. Rocked. Waited. What was taking the park rangers so long to hike out to the falls and return with some news? Dangling her legs over the foot bridge toward the creek near the parking lot, she tore another pine needle off a branch and tossed it into the water.

"Miss James?"

Helene jumped and rotated to look at the sneaky officer. "Yes?"

"There's nothing there."

"What?" How could that be? She'd seen the body. It couldn't be her mind playing tricks on her. Not this time. It was so real. "Are you sure?"

"Yes, ma'am."

She recognized the look in his eyes. A bit wary, as if she might lash out at him any second. A bit sympathetic, as if she were a sick child. A bit irritated, as if she were a liar. She jerked to her feet. "You have to look again." Her voice was rising too quickly, becoming too shrill. She tried to tone it down, to rope it back in. "Please. I know what I saw."

He raised one eyebrow. "Are you sure, Helene?"

He knew. He'd pulled her ID, and he knew all about her. Helene struggled to fit her numb arms through the backpack straps.

"Let me help you." He reached toward her.

She yanked away. "I'm fine. I know what I saw. You may not believe me, but someone was there."

He nodded, his lips compressed into a tight, ugly little line. "We can help you get home or to the hospital—"

"I'm fine!" Helene's heart rate sped as she made her way to her car. She wasn't fine. She needed Bob. Too bad her cell phone wouldn't work to call her emergency therapist until she was out of the Smoky Mountain National Park and back into the real world.

"Ma'am, you can't leave."

He reached for her again. She shrugged him off and backed away, her back pressing into the bridge's board railing. "Don't touch me!" A splinter worked its way through her shirt, digging into her hip, grounding her to the situation at hand. She wasn't crazy. She wasn't crazy. She wasn't—

Images danced in her periphery. Children taunting her. Medical staff closing in, their outstretched blue-gloved hands reaching for her. The leather restraints closing off circulation to her toes and fingertips. No! She wouldn't go back there.

Not again.

Not ever again.

The park ranger took a step closer. His mouth moved, but his words were lost in the few feet between them, falling from his lips like drops of liquid music notes. Floating away on the creek's high tide below her. She turned to watch them dance down the waves, bits of vibrantly colored lines and dots and curlicues swimming with the fishes.

His hot hand touched her shoulder, and she flinched. "Don't touch me!"

"Ma'am…"

His garbled voice refused to make sense in her ears. She needed Bob.

"…hospital…"

"No!" In one fluid motion, Helene leaped over the railing and plunged into the creek below. The icy cold mountain water stole her breath. She surfaced and gasped.

The park ranger's face above her said it all. His hanging-open mouth no longer spoke, but the look screamed at her.

You're crazy, Helene. And you know it. No sense fighting the inevitable. She allowed her body to fall limply into the water. They'd retrieve her and take her to the hospital, or they wouldn't and she would be Home soon.

Chapter Two

Zach intertwined his fingers with Annalise's. She smiled at him. It still felt weird. She had to admit. Friends their whole lives turned romantic still felt weird. No doubt about it. Especially at work. She pulled her hand back. Hurt flashed across his eyes. "Sorry, it just... feels unprofessional while we're on the clock."

He nodded.

"I'll make it up to you later."

Zach's eyebrows shot upward.

Oh, sheesh. Heat suffused her cheeks. "Not like that. I meant, um, I'm fixing meatloaf for dinner for you tonight."

He chuckled. "My favorite."

She sighed. That was awkward too. It had only been a few weeks since they'd decided to cross the "I love you like that" line. Surely, they would figure it out soon. Right?

"Cades Cove again."

Bless him for changing the subject. "Yeah, I'm starting to wonder if I'll feel differently about this place soon."

"Missing woman, now missing body. I hope there's not a pattern here."

Where was the normal Zach humor? The teasing, changing of subjects, giving-her-a-hard-time bestie she'd become accustomed to? She sighed again. "Me too."

Zach turned the SUV onto the gravel road leading to Abram's Falls.

She waved at the park ranger standing guard, keeping motorists from entering the area. Harold, maybe? She recognized his face from their last adventure here, but the name pulled away just out of reach. "I heard from Olivia yesterday."

"Oh, yeah?"

"She and the family are doing so well. It's been such a relief to know the Juarez Cartel has come to its last and final end." She hoped. Would their reign of terror always niggle the back of her mind? Probably. After burning her house down, nearly killing her ex-partner and friend Olivia, attacking her, and finding out Zach's father was the ringleader, how could it not?

"Where'd you go?"

She flashed a fake smile Zach's direction. "Nowhere. Just thinking."

"I don't believe you." He grinned. "But I'll let this one slide, since you're making meatloaf and all."

She giggled. "Gee, thanks."

He put the vehicle in Park, and they climbed out.

"Oh, look, there's Blu." Annalise waved at the handsome park ranger they'd met on the Beck case.

"Great."

She elbowed Zach's side. "Be nice."

"He likes you. How can I be nice?"

"He does not. He's just nice."

Zach shrugged. "I'll do my best."

"Boys, I swear. They get bigger, but they never grow up." She rolled her eyes and smiled up at him, pulling him to a stop before they reached the circle of waiting rangers. "Zach, look at me."

His gaze dropped to hers.

"I'm yours. It doesn't matter if he likes me or not."

A grin burst across his lips. "And you can cook. I'm a lucky man."

"Don't forget it." She spun on her heels and marched to the group. Zach's footsteps crunched in the gravel behind her. "Hi, Blu. Can you get us up to speed?"

"Hi, Annalise. It's good to see you." He leaned in for a hug.

Annalise stepped back and stuck her hand out.

He paused, shook it, and quirked an eyebrow. "Well, Helene James was hiking the Falls trail and claims she saw a body sunk in the pool beneath Abram's."

"And?"

"When we arrived, there was no one there. But you'd already been called, so we thought we'd wait for you to get here. I really don't think there's anything to investigate." His voice dropped to a whisper. "Other than her mental health. She has a history."

Annalise did not like the tone in his voice. She bored him with a steely gaze. "What kind of history?"

"Schizophrenia."

"So you think she hallucinated seeing the body? Is that what I'm gathering?"

Blu nodded. "Bodies don't disappear."

"Except when they do. Where's Miss James?"

He pointed to an athletically-built woman on the footbridge over the creek.

"Thanks."

Zach leaned in close as they walked away from Blu. "Annalise, what was that all about?"

"It isn't fair to dismiss her just because she's unwell."

"I hate to say it, but Blu has a point. Depending on how extensive and advanced her schizophrenia is, isn't it possible she imagined the whole thing?"

Annalise crossed her arms over her chest and stopped on the pine-needle-coated trail. "I suppose."

"All I'm saying is, don't assume anything." He brushed his fingers against her biceps.

Electricity shot up her arm. She shivered, and for a moment her mind wandered to places it shouldn't go. She reined it back in, shaking her head and frowning, but she knew he was right. Would her levelheadedness ever return? What was wrong with her these last months?

Divorce.

Cheating ex-husband who said awful things about her.

Being forced to shoot, and kill, Zach's father.

Right. Only those minor three things.

"Come on." Zach's sympathetic smile washed over her.

He knew how she struggled. He knew how she thought. What better partner or new boyfriend could she ask for? She relaxed her shoulders and forced a smile. "Right. Do me a favor?"

"Sure."

"Don't assume anything"

"Touché." He grinned. "I'll try. For you."

"Excuse us, please, gentleman." Annalise motioned for them to step away while they interviewed Miss James.

The two rangers shrugged and meandered back to where Blu waited.

Annalise smiled. "Miss James, I am Special Agent Annalise Baker. This is Special Agent Leebow. Can you tell us, in as much detail as possible, exactly what you saw?"

Helene frowned and pulled the brown wool blanket tighter around her shoulders. "You aren't going to believe me either, are you?"

What had those rangers said to this woman? "Ma'am, I will believe facts. What did you see?"

Helene bit her bottom lip. "She was just lying there. At the bottom."

Annalise drew in a breath when Helene paused.

"The sunlight streamed through the water, like it was dancing on her skin."

"Do you remember what she was wearing?"

"Blue jeans and a green t-shirt. She was face down, so I couldn't see if it said anything."

An awful lot of detail for imagination. "Anything else?"

Water dripped from the tips of Helene's multicolored hair as she seemed to search her memory. "A bracelet. I remember it sparkling as the wind blew and the leaves shifted, letting the sunshine bounce off it."

Zach spoke up. "Hair color?"

Helene's eyes shifted toward him. "Brown."

Annalise made a note of it. "What happened after you saw the victim?"

"I ran back here, flagged down a passing park ranger, and told him what happened." Helene crossed her arms. "They didn't find anything, so of course they think I am lying or crazy."

"No one thinks you're crazy, Miss James. We are just trying to figure out exactly what's happening here."

"I think she's crazy," Zach mumbled as he got into the SUV.

"Zachary!" She slapped his arm.

"What? Bodies don't just disappear." He sighed. There he went again, sounding like that jerk Blu. "Never mind. Listen, if she really saw a body in the water, where did it go? Who moved it, way out in the middle of nowhere? How did the coincidental timing of her seeing the body and then it vanishing just so happen to happen?" Slick. "Doesn't her mental illness play a part in this at all?"

"Maybe it does. But we haven't even been to the falls yet. Maybe these guys missed something?"

"Blu miss something? He's too perfect for that." His tone held much more bite than he'd intended.

"She is sick, but she could be correct. You don't know yet."

"Annalise, you believe all our witnesses. Even when they don't deserve your trust."

Annalise's nostrils flared. "You know what? I'll hike out there myself. If you're already convinced this is a waste of time, I'm happy to do our job for us. Alone."

She exited the SUV and slammed the door.

Ugh. Lovely. What was his deal?

Chapter Three

"It'll be dark in an hour," Zach commented from nearby.

She shrugged. They'd hiked in silence. She still wasn't ready to open her mouth. If she did, words would gush out she didn't necessarily mean and couldn't take back. Things had been so tense between them since she'd been forced to shoot his father. Had it really been six weeks ago? The nightmares and... daymares... was that a word?... had been enough to stretch the month and a half to a lifetime.

"See anything?"

She shook her head and caught a glimpse of her reflection in the water's edges. The dark bags under her eyes showed her the toll her conscience was taking on her.

"Come on, Annalise. Aren't you ever going to speak to me again?"

She spun and slammed her fists to her hips. "What do you want me to say? Huh? That you hurt my feelings? That I'm sorry, again, for killing your father? That I'm sorry my gut has been off for months now and that I'm not sure it'll ever be back to normal?" Tears burned her eyes. She swallowed and tried to force them to stay put. "That I'm scared our friendship just got ruined because we crossed a line we can't uncross? That I'm scared you'll stop loving me because I'm not the same woman I was? That—"

Zach took three bounding steps toward her and wrapped her in his arms. "Annalise, stop. I'm sorry. So sorry." He kissed the top of her head. "You're amazing. I'm the one who was wrong."

For a moment, she savored the comfort his arms offered. "We have work to do."

"We will work through it all. Together. I promise."

How could he promise that? How could he know, be so certain, he wanted her after all she'd done? "I'm sorry, Zach. I hate that I'm the one who had to pull that trigger on your father."

"I know. I do too."

Because he saw her differently now? Because he'd always hold a grudge? She sniffled and pushed free. "I'm going to the far side."

He nodded. "I'll search up top."

"Deal." Good. She needed some space to regain composure.

Annalise skipped across the rocks, landing on the far side, somehow still dry. If the slimy rocks had their say, she'd have been in the drink after the first step. She forced all the issues swirling in her head to the side and studied each patch of ground, both in and out of the creek. Thankfully, the water was so clean that the bottom, filled with smooth stones and red-orange Tennessee clay, shimmered clearly in the dimming light.

Clear enough to show her there was nothing. Not a single piece of evidence. Anywhere. Maybe Helene really was losing her mind? Maybe the woman had daymares too.

"Annalise!"

She jerked her gaze toward him.

"I'm calling it. There's nothing here."

He was calling it? All by himself? Just deciding there was nothing and not even asking her opinion. Heat scalded her veins. She bit her tongue. The sky was growing darker by the second. She nodded. A good night's rest wouldn't hurt anyone, and if she had to finish searching tomorrow by herself, she would.

The phone jarred Annalise awake. For once, she'd been sleeping soundly. "Hello?"

"Ms. Baker?"

"Yes."

"This is Helene."

Annalise slid to a sitting position and glanced at her bedside clock. Three a.m. Lovely. "Yes, ma'am. How can I help you?"

"Were you asleep?" Helene sighed. "Of course you were asleep. It's the middle of the night."

Annalise drew a deep breath and forced the grogginess from her voice. "It's okay. Is there something you needed?"

"No… Yes… I mean, I just hoped you'd found something."

"No, ma'am. Unfortunately not. However, I am planning to head back over there in the morning." Well, later in the morning. You know, when the sun came up.

"Oh."

"Are you all right, Miss James?"

"Yes… No… I don't know."

Annalise's gut clenched. That was super reassuring. "Where are you?"

"Home." Helene's voice climbed several octaves. "I'm fine."

Hysteria wasn't far from the fringes of Helene's words. "I'm going to call and have an ambulance come check on you, okay?"

"No!" Helene cleared her throat. "I mean no. I'm fine. I promise."

Annalise had more than one doubt about that. "I really think someone should check on you, ma'am. Is there anyone you can call?"

"I'm fine!" Helene screeched.

"I'm sending someone over, Miss James. Just to be sure."

The line went dead. As she pulled on her clothes and boots, Annalise flipped her laptop open and found Helene's address on their report form from earlier. She dialed 9-1-1 and requested they dispatch an ambulance and police officer to Helene's residence. Annalise darted out the door and drove faster than she should to the apartment outside Pigeon Forge. *Lord, please help Helene. She is struggling, and, even though I don't know her, I'm worried.*

Multicolored lights reflecting from the buildings alerted her to EMS's presence before she entered the complex. In the early morning fog, other apartment residents gathered in the parking lot, giving the place a cinema-like quality. She parked and stepped out of her SUV to find an eerie silence, enhanced by the strobing, pulsating, make-her-head-ache lights.

Annalise climbed the stairs. At Helene's door, a paramedic nearly bowled her over. "Excuse me."

"Ma'am, you can't be up here."

She flashed her badge. "I'm Special Agent Annalise Baker. I'm the one who called. Helene James is a witness in a potential homicide."

The man's gruff exterior whisked away as his shoulders drooped. "She's barricaded herself in the bathroom and is threatening suicide if we don't leave, which is why we can't leave. Obviously." He rolled his eyes. "Perhaps you can talk some sense into her."

Annalise's heart clenched. Poor woman! She was probably scared out of her mind right about now. *Lord?* Annalise couldn't finish the prayer and hoped He knew exactly what Helene needed.

An officer with a deep frown waited at the bathroom door. He opened his mouth, but Annalise cut him off. "Special Agent Annalise Baker. I know her." Was know too strong a word? She had only met Helene a few hours ago.

The officer relaxed. "She's refusing to come out. Threatening suicide if we don't all leave."

Annalise nodded. "I know. Paramedic told me. Mind if I try talking to her?"

"Be my guest." He waved his hand and retreated farther down the hallway.

Annalise knocked softly. "Helene? It's Agent Baker."

"You called them! After I said I was okay!"

"I know, Helene. I did. I'm sorry. I was worried about you."

There was a long pause. "You were worried about me?"

"Yes. You seemed so upset on the phone and earlier today at the hike."

Another pause, and then Annalise heard a dull thump against the door. Was Helene leaning on the other side now? "I want to help you, Helene."

"That's what they all say. Then I end up strapped to a bed, doped out of my head to the point I can't think straight. And then they expect me to just be their good little patient, even though they don't want to know how I really feel. They don't care that I hate the way their meds make me feel and that I want to be better but not like that... not like that..."

Annalise bit her lip. What on earth could she say to that? Where had Zoe's mom gone for treatment when life had overwhelmed her? Annalise tried to pull the details from the fuzzy recesses of her mind. It had been so long ago. Friends in third grade, Annalise had only been allowed to go to Zoe's house one time before Mom and Dad said it wasn't safe. "Helene, I may have an idea. I know you don't want to go back to that place." Wherever that place was. "What if we find somewhere that's better?"

"They're all awful, Miss Baker. Trust me."

Could that be true? "I don't know how else to help. Clearly, you aren't well." Annalise held her breath.

"I'm not crazy."

She exhaled deeply, massaging her temples. "I did not say that. I don't believe you're crazy. Not in the least."

"You don't?"

"No. I do believe you need some extra help getting well though."

"Yeah, maybe."

"I can't promise everything will be okay. I can, however, promise I will come check on you and that I will do everything I can to help you."

"You will?"

"I promise."

The door cracked open. Helene peered out, tears streaking her face. "She was there, Miss Baker. I swear she was."

"I believe you, Helene. I believe you."

Zach's alarm clock woke him from a fitful sleep. He cracked his eyelids and slammed them shut again as the bathroom light stabbed his retinas. Too early. His phone chimed almost as soon as he hit snooze.

"Going to Cades Cove. See you later today—Lise."

What? Zach bolted upright, knocking his comforter to the floor. He shot back a reply, "Wait for me." He rushed through his morning routine, which consisted of very little anyway, he supposed. And ran out the front door. Was she seriously going to hike to Abram's Falls solo? He chuckled. This was Annalise, he was thinking about. Master hiker. Outdoorswoman extraordinaire. She would be fine.

He still wanted her to wait for him.

They were partners. And in a relationship. Ugh. The last several weeks had been difficult. He could imagine she needed some space from his grief. He was stuck in the anger phase of the cycle. He needed some space from it himself.

Half an hour later, with bagels and coffee in the passenger seat, he pulled into Annalise's driveway. Her beagle, Millie, raced out to bark and wag her tail at him. He peered up at the early-morning-sun-laden deck and waited for Annalise's gorgeous face to appear and smile down at him as she had so many mornings before. With that little half-wave and the self-conscious flip of the ponytail or tug of the ball cap, the woman melted his heart every time. He exhaled the breath he'd been holding when she didn't appear. Strange.

As he exited the vehicle, he patted Millie's head, and she licked his hand. "Good morning, sweet girl. Whatcha been up to this morning? Huh?"

Millie's tail wagged even harder, then she raced to the front door.

Zach followed and swung it open to allow her passage. Annalise sat on the couch in front of the massive hearth, laptop open, and a scowl on her face. He leaned over the back of the couch and kissed her on the top of the head. "Morning."

She jumped. "Hey. Sorry."

He chuckled. "What're you so engrossed in?"

"It's a long story. Come on. I'll tell you on the way."

Though Annalise's words were hurried and her voice chipper, the bags under her eyes told another story. "Have you slept?"

"Some."

"How much coffee have you had?"

She tilted her head sideways and grinned. "Some?"

"Oh, right. I'll bet. More like tons."

She moved toward the front door, but he intercepted her with a gentle tug of her wrist. She spun to face him, and he caught her in his arms, hugging her close. He kissed her forehead. "Are we okay?"

Her eyebrows knitted together. "We will be, Zach. We always are, aren't we?"

A knot released in his chest. "I love you."

"I love you too." She pulled back. "Now come on. We've got work to do."

"We do?" Was there a new case he didn't know about? Or... oh... of course. Having Annalise in his arms had driven out all of yesterday for a moment. "You mean the missing slash nonexistent body?"

She frowned. "Missing. I believe Helene."

He sighed. That was one of the reasons he loved her. Her faith in people. Her belief in things always turning out for the best. It balanced his pessimism well, but this time Annalise might be disappointed. She'd been off her game since her divorce, since she realized life was out of her control, and especially since she'd shot his father. A zing of anger flashed through him. He took a deep breath and forced the feeling aside. "I'm with you. On your side, as usual." He faked a smile he didn't feel past his lips and followed her to the truck.

Chapter Four

Sweat poured down Annalise's back, tickling her shoulders as it rolled over them. She swiped her forehead against her sleeve and sucked down another large gulp of cool water. "It's hot."

Zach chuckled on the trail behind her. "Yes, it is."

"Almost there, though."

"Yep."

"Where was I?"

"You were telling me about the medics."

"Oh, right. They were so rude to Helene. They treated her like she wasn't able to process anything they said."

"That's awful."

"I couldn't believe it. She was so scared, but she went anyway. Thank goodness. I'm worried about her."

"You barely know her, Annalise."

"I'm still worried." As a Christian, wasn't that her duty? Both as a child of God and a servant of the community, she had vowed to help people. "I believe her. Plus, she doesn't seem to have anyone on her side."

"You have such a big heart." He pulled her to a stop and wrapped his arms around her shoulders. "It's one of the things I admire about you."

"Thanks."

"But—"

"Zach, let's not argue again. Please."

He released her. "I was just going to say, be careful about getting your hopes up. I hate seeing you hurt."

She stepped onto the rocky, muddy stream bank next to Abram's Falls, where the trail ended and water took over and erased human intentions to subdue wilderness. "I'll try. And thank you. I know you do." He'd seen a lot of her hurting lately. She didn't particularly enjoy it much herself. "As soon as we get back out of here today, I'm calling Haven House. I'm glad you knew what I was talking about when I mentioned it earlier."

"Yeah, me too." He drew a sip of water from his backpack straw. "Okay, where do we start?"

"Well, I read Blu's report when I couldn't sleep this morning. Helene had told them she'd 'seen the body under the water near the far side, just south of the largest rock.' I'll hop over there. You stay here and scan the shallows again. Deal?"

He nodded.

"Thanks, Zach. I'm glad you're always on my side."

"Since the sandbox."

She giggled. "Exactly." If she closed her eyes and played through those early memories, she could still see his cute, little, blond head backing down that bully for her. Sand on his fingertips and under his nails, a bright yellow dump truck in one hand, and a frown on his face. And every crossroads, hard time, down-in-the-dumps moment since, he'd been there. On her side.

Annalise made her way to the approximate location she guessed Helene had seen the body and peered into the clear water. Ripples from the fall clouded the surface, but she could still make out most details of the bottom, where smooth, moss-covered river stones lay in heaps, colored by sunlight in places and hiding in shadows in others. A trout fingerling flashed by, its silvery sides glistening in a patch of golden light. And something else sparkled there. In the crevice between two stones. What was that? "Zach! I think I see something!"

"Coming!" His words were nearly drowned out by the rush of the fall to her right.

She slipped off her boots, rolled up her pants legs, and waded in. The icy, mountain-fed water bit her bare toes and ankles, and the floor dropped more quickly than she imagined it would. A few steps later, it didn't matter that she'd rolled her pants legs up. Gripping a rock with her left foot, and her arms spread wide, Annalise stretched and tried to wiggle her toes of the other foot into the crevice where the shiny object waited. She'd picked things off the floor with her toes for as long as she could remember. But this tiny little thing refused to be manipulated by toe-power.

"Whaddya got?" Zach asked from the shore nearest.

"Not sure—" As Annalise turned to answer him, her feet slid on the slimy bottom. The cold water zapped her breath as she plopped onto her rear. Hard. Laughter spilled from her along with chills as the iciness soaked her shirt up to her armpits. "Brrr…"

Zach chuckled and reached for her, but he was too far by several inches.

"Hang on." She groped the soft mud beneath her until her fingers felt the foreign object. A bracelet? She held it up for Zach to see. "It has an inscription on the back, *Corinne*, and a heart."

"Interesting." He held his hand out again, this time balancing on a rock and stretching even farther to reach out.

She grabbed his hand.

He steadily pulled her to her feet.

Her teeth chattered as she stood next to him on the larger rock and let the water run in rivulets from her clothing. Zach wrapped his arm around her shoulder and snugged her close to his side. "I'll warm up soon. It's too hot to stay cold."

"Right. Especially with the coming hike."

She heard him, but her thoughts weren't on getting back. She turned the bracelet again and again in her hands. Other than the name inscribed on the gold, there was nothing significant. It could've come from any hiker at any point in time. But Helene had mentioned seeing what she thought was a bracelet on the body. "Let's check the forest on this side, since we didn't have a chance yesterday before dark."

"Whatever you say, boss lady."

She quirked a smile his direction. "You're lucky I don't shove you in, Mr. Sarcastic."

"Might feel good, right about now."

"Oh, really?" Annalise nudged Zach's side with her elbow. He tottered but didn't lose his balance. Not that she truly wanted him to, but part of her kind of wished she nudged a bit harder.

"Hey, now." He smiled and held his palms out. "No more boss comments." His shining eyes danced as he darted them to the side and bit his lip. "Though now that we are dating, doesn't that mean you are the boss? Women are always right, right?"

"Oh, ho! That does it. In you go!" She playfully pushed his shoulders.

His eyes grew wide as he flopped backward into the water. He came up spluttering and swiping water from his forehead. "You didn't!"

Annalise squealed as he plunged toward her. She tucked the bracelet into her pocket just as he wrapped his arms around her waist and pulled her back into the water. She came up spitting water and giggling, his warm, strong arms pulling her close. In an instant, all joviality vanished. The look in his eye, the smoldering, dark intensity zapped her strength and tingled all the way to her toenail tips. Her breath caught in her throat as he leaned in. How could his kisses elicit such fire from her?

Breathless, she pulled away. "We have… work to do, mister."

"Yes." He cleared his throat, but his voice remained husky. "Yes, I suppose that's true."

Under his scrutiny, she blushed. "What?"

"You're beautiful, Annalise."

She dipped her chin. "Thank you. You're not so bad yourself."

He puffed out his chest. "Purty as a peacock."

"Whatever." Her laughter bounced off the rocks around them and skidded across the surface of the water. "Come on. I still want to take a gander in the woods over yonder."

"I love it when you speak hick."

"I figured since you were comparing yourself to a bird and all... get it, gander?"

He chuckled. "So clever." He helped steady her as she climbed out of the creek, and she let him. He'd always had a streak of protectiveness over her, but it was different now. Gentler. More intimate. She wasn't yet used to it, but she'd sure like to get there.

Work. He had to focus on the task at hand. Not at the soaking-wet, skin-clinging-clothed, beautiful woman a few steps ahead of him. Man! Kisses like that, like all of them with her, were enough to drive a man to distraction every moment of every day. Including this moment. What was he supposed to be looking for again?

Oh, right. Clues. To the missing/nonexistent body. Not Annalise's shapely one...

"Zach?"

He jerked his gaze to her face. "Hmmm?"

"You with me here?"

Was he ever. Just not in the way he was supposed to be probably. "Sort of. What's up?"

"Look." She pointed firmly at the ground.

Four-wheeler tracks. "Strange."

"Yeah. I thought so too. Let's radio Blu and see if they've had a reason to be out here on the ATVs recently."

"Maybe they came out to look when Helene reported yesterday?"

She shook her head. "No, they hiked. Remember?"

"Right."

Annalise retrieved her backpack where it lay on a large rock and depressed the button on the walkie-talkie attached to the strap. "SMIF to Cades Cove Ranger Station."

"Go ahead, Agent Baker. This is Ranger Blu."

Annalise smiled.

Zach frowned. Even hearing Blu's voice irritated him.

"Hey, Blu. Have you guys been on ATVs out here, other side of Abram's lately? Probably right before the last rain."

"Hang on, pretty lady. I'll check."

Zach growled. Just nice, his foot.

Blu's voice crackled through the radio again. "Nothing on the books. I didn't think there should've been but just wanted to be sure, Annalise. There's ATV tracks or something out there?"

"Yep. They are at most a couple days old now."

"Okay, come on into the station, and we'll look at maps together."

Together? Why did Blu have to insert that particular word?

"Will do, Blu. Thanks."

Blu and Annalise sidled up, shoulder to shoulder, giggling and—not how he wanted to spend the rest of his day. Since when was he so jealous? Oh, that was right. Since Blu showed up a few weeks ago, flirted with his best friend turned girlfriend, and since he saw how Annalise reacted to said flirting.

"Let's follow these a little ways and see which direction they head."

Zach tuned back into the current situation to find Annalise squatted over the four-wheeler imprints, her brow wrinkled. "We aren't equipped to hike backwoods today." He groaned. "Maybe we should just head back to the ranger station and see what Blu wants."

"I really want to see where these head, Zach. I've got a hunch."

A hunch? Why couldn't she just, for once, listen to him? "Annalise, we can't go gallivanting into the forest this morning. We only have enough water for this hike. No emergency supplies." What was she thinking? She was usually the voice of reason. Maybe her natural instincts were worn away after her divorce and months of self-doubt... She did shoot his father— What was he thinking? This was Annalise. If she shot his father, it was because there was no other choice. Not to mention, good ole Dad was the ringleader for one of the most notorious drug scandals in Tennessee history. Zach sighed. How long was the anger stage of grief supposed to last?

Chapter Five

Annalise scooched back as Blu leaned in. Again. The smell of his cologne, Abercrombie and Fitch, if she remembered correctly from her high school mall-hanging-out days, overpowered her. Water still dripped a small puddle from her not-quite-dry clothes, and her boots squelched as she shifted position.

He smiled and met her gaze as he pointed to the logbook on his desk. "No one has been out there in the last three months on the ATVs. You sure that's what you saw?"

Annalise resisted the urge to roll her eyes. His rugged handsomeness couldn't outweigh his personality. "I'm sure, Blu. Four-wheeler tracks headed northeast, directly into the forest."

"Hmmm." He tapped his chin. "I don't know why, unless someone was scouting for hunting outside the park boundaries and got turned around."

Again, her eyes wanted to roll, and it almost hurt to stop them. "It's a pretty good piece to the nearest allowable hunting, isn't it?"

"It is. But who knows? I can't see why anyone would be out there on ATVs otherwise."

She could think of at least a half-dozen reasons. Drugs. Moonshine. Kidnapping. She'd seen all three in the last six months. Plus, poaching, murder, and plain old rabblerousing. She snickered. Who used the word rabblerousing anymore? "Okay, think there's any chance we can get an aerial search of the area?"

He crossed his arms over his chest and frowned. "Wouldn't count on it. Not without a verified missing person or at least some evidence of a crime."

That's what she figured. Missing person? Duh! She hadn't even looked at the NamUs database yet. She'd been so focused on Helene and the waterfall search… "Come on, Zach."

His eyebrows shot up. "Something on your mind?"

"I'll tell you on the way. Thanks, Blu." She tossed the words over her shoulder as she exited the small building.

Twenty minutes later, they pulled into SMIF headquarters. Annalise hopped out, grabbed her laptop bag from the back seat of her SUV, and made her way through the building toward the shade garden out back. She did her best thinking outdoors.

"Need help?" Zach shouted at her retreating form.

"Nah. I'm good. I'll let you know what I find."

Outside, under the boughs of a gnarly-branched sweetgum, Annalise breathed deeply. *Please let this work, Lord.* She pulled the bracelet from her pocket and entered the name into the National Missing and Unidentified Persons database. The swirling circle icon told her it was looking and looking…and looking. "Oh, hurry up already."

Finally, the search returned one entry.

Missing since Friday, June 5, 2020, Corinne Porter. Last seen wearing blue jeans and a green shirt, 5'7" tall, brown hair, 155 pounds. Please call Scott County Police Department if you have any information.

Three weeks? Annalise's heart hammered out of her chest as she entered headquarters. "Hey, guys. I found something." The name matched. The clothing matched. There was too much coincidence to be coincidence.

Kirk and Zach emerged from their offices.

"You okay?" Concern etched Zach's brow.

She nodded. She was right. There was a case. But that also meant there was a body. And someone's sister, daughter, friend, wife, lover was dead.

Chapter Six

"We need an aerial search." Annalise tapped her toe on the floor.

Kirk held his hands up. "Wait, Annalise. Now, we need more than a bracelet to call THP in on this one. How do you know the family didn't hike here at some point and lose the bracelet then?"

"And," Zach interjected, "we don't have any information. At all."

Annalise huffed. "Fine." They were right, of course, but it irked her. "I'll call the family."

"Thank you," Kirk said.

"If I get an affirmative that they've never been here, can we request aerial then?"

Kirk nodded.

Annalise spun toward her desk and grabbed her cell. She dialed the number for Scott County PD given in the NamUS result. "I have information regarding Corinne Porter."

"Oh, yes, ma'am. Hang on a minute. I'll transfer you."

A few seconds of silence later, a female answered. "This is Officer Denton. How may I help you?"

Annalise explained her suspicions. "I need to get in contact with the family."

The excitement in Officer Denton's voice rang clearly through. "Of course, Special Agent." She sighed. "But I will caution you. We have had so many leads that were bogus. I don't want to get these folks' hopes up. Their daughter is all they have, and they've been devastated since she's been missing."

"I understand." She bit her lip. If she left now, she could be in Scott County in two hours. "Probably better to visit in person, eh? Rather than call?"

"I'd say so, ma'am."

"I'll meet you at your station at three."

"I'll be waiting."

Annalise shot up the interstate, windows down, hot summer air whipping her ponytail against her neck and ears. Zach wasn't happy to be left behind, but Kirk needed help with files, and Annalise needed a break. Seemed she'd needed a lot of those lately. Why? She'd never needed them before, when they were just friends, when they were still normal, when they were on solid ground. Ugh. She sighed and rolled her eyes at her reflection in the rearview. Was she bound to overthink every minute of every day of her life?

Hadn't she settled anything with Him last time they'd had that one-on-one when He'd told her to trust Him to handle this thing called life?

Apparently not.

She cranked up the old Dolly song on the radio and tried to force her mind to the upcoming meeting. Much easier to focus on murder than her relationship with Zach—or Him.

A couple hours later, Annalise pulled under the awning in front of the Oneida Police Department's main entrance. Like most small towns, the police department matched the surrounding buildings, brick, tin roof. Small. A pang warmed her chest. She missed Norris Police Department at times like this. The camaraderie, the laid-back feel, the "justice reigns supreme" mentality, and especially working for Captain Brooks. She needed to call him and check in. Last she heard, everyone was enjoying summer break, and he'd taken the guys on a backcountry camping trip.

A female officer about Annalise's height exited the station door. Annalise stepped from her SUV and smiled. "You must be Officer Denton. How are you?"

"Anxious. You sure this lead's solid?"

"As sure as I can be, ma'am." Did Denton know the victim's family personally? That would explain her intense emotion to the situation. "Why don't you ride with me, and I'll explain everything I know so far on the way?"

Officer Denton frowned but nodded slowly. "All right. Let me grab my things."

Annalise sighed. Clearly, Officer Denton didn't trust Annalise. This was going to be a long drive, and she didn't even know how far away they lived.

A moment or two later, Officer Denton settled into the passenger seat, patted her sidearm, and placed her bag on the floor between her feet. Was she going through a mental list? Maybe an escape plan if Annalise's driving wasn't up to par? Annalise forced her lips to remain neutral. "So, can you tell me anything about the Porters?"

"They're a good Christian family. We've gone to church together since I can remember. It shocked us all when Corinne disappeared."

Annalise's instincts about the situation had been right. Denton knew the victim's family very well, it sounded like. "Where was she last seen?"

"Well, Mom and Pop Porter—everyone calls them that—live on the mountain up here to the left." Denton pointed at a turn.

Annalise took it.

"Corinne lived in an apartment in the Old City in Knoxville. She's a graduate from UT and works in their library." Denton cleared her throat. "Worked."

There was pain in that one word. Intentionally hidden, forcefully clamped down pain. "I'm sorry for your loss here too, Officer Denton."

"Call me Katie, please."

"Katie, then. I know this has to be hard."

She nodded. "I'm trying to remain objective."

Annalise knew all about that. Images of Zach's father leaning into the wrecked truck, assaulting Olivia, and then falling backward as the bullets from Annalise's gun plunged into his chest filled her mind's eye.

Katie was still talking. "Corinne was last seen walking home from the UT library. Something she'd done a million times."

A million times. The same route probably. Had someone watched her? Planned out a kidnapping? Or was it spur-of-the-moment?

"Turn again here." Katie pointed to the right. "Just up there, third drive on the left."

Annalise followed the instructions and wound up a gravel driveway to a farmhouse perched in the middle of a small clearing. It was like it had grown from the side of the bluff above it, a beautiful addition to the rugged landscape with its massive windows and sharp angles. "Wow, it's amazing. Like a treehouse on the ground."

"Pop Porter designed and built it himself. Wait till you see the inside."

Annalise parked next to an old Ford pickup that shined in the afternoon sunlight and hopped out. She followed Katie to the front door.

An older woman answered Katie's knock. "Hey, Mom Porter. This is Special Agent Baker. She'd like to talk to you about Corinne."

Mrs. Porter's face blanched. "Come in."

Annalise entered the front door and gazed at the décor. Woodsy, a touch of magic, with oil paintings and watercolors of flowers and trails and trees decorating each nook and cranny. "Are you the artist?"

Mrs. Porter nodded. "Have a seat. Would you like some tea?"

"No thank you, ma'am." Annalise smiled. "They're beautiful."

"Thank you." Mrs. Porter nodded and grabbed a dish towel from the back of one of the kitchen chairs. She wrung it between her hands. "You have bad news."

It wasn't a question. And the barely-checked tears shaking her voice said Mrs. Porter already knew her daughter was gone. "We have a potential lead. I cannot verify with one-hundred-percent accuracy that it is related to your daughter." Annalise pulled the bracelet from her pocket, now encased in a plastic evidence bag. "Is this Corinne's?"

Tears sprang to Mrs. Porter's eyes. "Yes. It was a gift from her pop on her nineteenth birthday. She never took it off."

Annalise's heart ached for this woman. "Do you know if Corinne had ever hiked the Abram's Falls trail in Cades Cove?"

"Oh, yes, many times. In fact, they just took the youth group there about a month ago. Maybe six weeks?" Mrs. Porter looked to Katie, who nodded.

"I couldn't go. Had to work that day, but Corinne said they had a wonderful time wading in the pool after a picnic. She loves the youth." Katie's chin dropped and her voice became a whisper, "Loved."

Mrs. Porter's hand flew to her dropping mouth. "That's it then? She truly is gone?"

Annalise's pulse thundered in her ears. "I'm sorry, Mrs. Porter."

"I want to see her body."

"We are still..." How did she finish that sentence? She'd intended to ease into this conversation and share all she knew from the least provocative details first.

Mrs. Porter squared her shoulders. "Then she could still be alive."

"We have a witness who saw who I now believe was your daughter at the bottom of Abram's Falls."

"I don't understand. If you have a witness who saw my sweet Corinne, why do you not now know where her body is?"

Annalise shifted her weight to the other foot. "Well, when park rangers returned, the victim's body was no longer there. But I found the bracelet the day after. I am hoping to mount a search as soon as I return." Would Blu and Kirk help her get a search knowing that Corinne had been there recently on a simple hiking trip?

"I see. I don't believe my daughter is dead. Find her. Do whatever it takes."

"I'll do my best, ma'am. But, please, try to remember there are multiple possible outcomes here and very few of them are ideal. It is a vast territory, rugged, nearly impassable in places."

"Find her, Special Agent. Bring my baby girl home to me. One way or another."

Chapter Seven

The next morning, Mrs. Porter's words weighed heavily on Annalise's mind and shoulders as she packed her hiking gear for a long haul into the Smokies. Millie paced at the foot of Annalise's bed. Poor pup knew her mom was leaving when the hiking pack came out of the closet. "It's okay, girl. I'll be back soon. Hopefully." Annalise stooped to massage the sweet beagle's ears. "Plus, you get to stay with Zach's mom for a day or two and see your buddy, Buddy."

Millie licked Annalise's hand and whined.

"I love you too."

Annalise had been tasked similarly to find first Cody and then Olivia, but, at least with their cases, there was a shred of hope they were alive.

And God had been on their side, the SMIF team being successful in the end bringing them both home safely to their families.

This was different. This was Helene already seeing Corinne's lifeless body. This was knowing it was recovery instead of rescue, pursuit of a murderer instead of a kidnapper. Both heinous but one with at least a potential for reunion this side of twilight.

She checked her email for the tenth time in an hour. Finally, a response from Haven for Hope awaited her.

"We would be happy to assist with your friend. Along with the recommendation from her psychiatrist, we have opened a room immediately for Helene James. Please fill out this information packet and advise patient to plan for a hospital transfer by ambulance to Haven for Hope later this afternoon."

Yes! Annalise sighed. Hopefully the team there could get Helene the inpatient help she needed, and Helene would be more comfortable.

She called Helene's hospital room. There was no answer. She left a message with the nurses at the front desk and got an email address to forward the paperwork to. Helene would have to help with that information. Annalise simply didn't know any of it.

A knock sounded at the front door, and Annalise jumped. "Sheesh, Millie-girl, what's my problem today?"

Millie ran out the bedroom door.

"Come in!"

A few moments later, Zach peeked around the corner. "'Bout ready?"

"Pretty close. Just gotta run Millie over to your mom's. Then we can head out. Kirk have everything in place for Blu and his team to meet us?"

Zach grinned.

"What?"

"He does. Blu was none too happy we want to do a grid search based on some random four-wheeler tracks."

Annalise rolled her eyes. "He'll get over it." She'd talked Kirk into the aerial search even though Corinne had been hiking near the falls. She could have lost the bracelet that day, but Helene was sure she'd seen it on Corinne's wrist. It was enough to try. Plus, she'd mentioned if they didn't do a full search, what with Annalise already notifying the family and all, someone would raise alarms and it would be a public affairs nightmare.

Zach kissed Annalise on the cheek. "That's my spunky girl."

She felt a blush creep into her cheeks. "Let me make a phone call."

Zach quirked an eyebrow, but he, surprisingly, kept his mouth closed.

Annalise dialed the number for Helene's hospital room again.

"Hello?" Helene sounded tired.

"Hi, it's Annalise Baker."

"Oh, hey. I'm glad you called. You said you would, and now you have. I'm glad."

Annalise smiled. "Me too. Listen, I wanted to update you. I found something in the falls that led me to a missing person's report. I have a team going into the woods this morning."

"That's great!" Helene coughed. "Okay, not great. But you know what I mean."

Annalise chuckled. "How are you doing?"

"I'm okay. I hate these medicines and IVs and doctors. And the lights. I really hate the lights. I just want to go home."

"I'm sure. But you've got to do what they tell you so you can go home when you're feeling better."

"Right. I know." She sighed. "I'm just so tired. And my friend won't stop talking nonstop."

Friend? "I'm so glad she's there to keep you company."

"Yeah…bye."

The line went dead before she'd had a chance to give Helene the good news about Haven for Hope. Annalise pulled the phone from her head. That was sudden. And strange. "Okay, Zach, I'm ready."

Leaning against her doorframe, a crooked smile on his lips, Annalise couldn't help but admire just how very handsome he was. For a minute anyway.

"What?"

She returned his devilish grin. "Nothin'. Just looking at you."

"Like what you see?"

She nodded. "It'll do in a pinch."

Zach's mouth dropped open. "In a pinch, huh?"

Annalise could hold the giggle in no longer, and when it erupted, Zach grabbed her in a bear hug and squeezed her to his chest. "I can't breathe, Zach."

He kissed her forehead and cheek and moved down to her neck. He placed one soft kiss at the nape and hovered there, his warm breath tickling her skin.

Annalise instantly stopped squirming. She couldn't breathe, now, if she wanted to. She cleared her throat. "Probably ought to get going."

"Yeah. Good idea." His husky tone underscored his words. He released her and backed out of the room.

Annalise steadied her quaking legs and slowed her rapid breathing. Whoa. Zach plus that kiss plus that bear hug was earth-shaking. Who would've imagined just a few short years ago they'd end up in this dynamic now? She hated that her divorce happened, but she couldn't exactly say she was sorry she and Zach were embarking on this new road together.

"Will the helicopter be in the air today?" she shouted in the general direction of her living room, where she figured Zach waited on her.

"S'posed to be. Blu's got them on standby waiting to hear from us."

"Good." Annalise entered the living room and pulled to a stop. Zach stood with his hands on his hips, back to her, at the front window. "You okay?"

"Um, yeah."

"Care to share what you're thinking?"

"Probably shouldn't." He spun and flashed one of his classic Zach grins.

She read it like a front-page article. The kiss had sent him spiraling too. "Love you."

"Love you too."

"Come on, partner. We've got work to do." They were going to figure this out. How to balance work and personal. How to forgive each other for hurtful words and thoughts over the last couple weeks. How to be best friends and be in love.

Chapter Eight

The blades of the helicopter swished overhead, and the rush of its engine dropped into the otherwise quiet forest. Zach walked a beeline about fifty feet from Annalise on one side, keeping his eyes trained on ground and girlfriend simultaneously. Blu searched on the other side. They trekked slowly through the trees and vegetation near Abram's Falls.

This all felt so familiar. How strange that they'd been on the other side of this valley just a few short weeks ago, doing a grid search for Olivia Beck.

Bless Annalise's beautiful, hopeful heart. If it wasn't for her, their first SMIF case, with Cody, would've ended with a dead child. Their second case with a permanently missing woman. And all their smaller cases in between without her ever-optimistic outlook would've been slogging-through miserable.

Was there truly a victim in this current case? He'd been so sure Helene was crazy. Yet, Annalise had chosen to believe. Her faith in people was so much stronger than his. Except for her faith in herself. He was going to help change that, if he could. If only she could see herself the way he saw her.

Guilt slithered into the back of his thoughts. He believed in her, but something still plagued him. How he longed to have a fly's glimpse into his father's shooting. Was there any other course of action she could've taken?

"Four-wheeler tracks start here." Annalise's words, lobbed over the spongy earth, made him glance toward her. She smiled.

He gave her a thumbs-up and then glanced toward the helicopter as it made another circling pass. The chances of finding anything, either on foot or by air, were slim—usually were in these cases—but he let himself allow a tiny bubble of hope to arise.

About twenty feet ahead, Zach spotted something snagged on a patch of tangled blackberry briars. What was that?

He stepped closer and unwound it. A piece of fabric. Possibly from a light green t-shirt? "Found something!"

Annalise jogged over. "What is it?"

He held the piece up.

Annalise nodded. "Could be hers."

"This could be from anyone passing through."

"True. But it could be from her." Annalise bit her lip. "What if she—"

"Wasn't dead?" Zach frowned. "Lise, don't go there. She was lifeless at the bottom of the pool. How exactly would she swim to the surface and walk away?"

The light in her eyes dimmed. "Right. You're right. Do you think it's possible a bear or mountain lion dragged her body from the water?"

He shrugged. "Maybe. Doesn't seem too likely. This has probably been here for a long time and doesn't even belong to her, but I'll bag it and GPS tag its location just in case."

"Air search to ground one," their radios crackled.

Annalise depressed the button. "Ground one, go ahead."

"We've spotted something northeast of the fall. About four miles."

"What?"

"Possibly a structure. Looks like someone's taken great efforts to disguise it."

Annalise waved Blu over as she pulled out a map. "Are there any old cabins or parts of the park history here?"

"Not that I'm aware of, but there are various buildings scattered everywhere. We find them from time to time."

She depressed the button once more, "Thanks, guys. We'll check it out."

Zach placed a halting hand on Annalise's forearm. "Four miles more and back will put us well into nighttime."

She tapped her backpack. "I'm prepared."

He quirked an eyebrow. Of course she was. "I'm not."

Annalise shrugged his hand off her arm. "I'm going, with or without you."

Heat rose in his chest. She could be so stubborn!

Blu chimed in, "My team is not prepared for an overnighter. We can continue the grid search here and let you know if we find anything else. But you'll be hiking the opposite direction, and we don't have anything more than this area planned."

Zach understood why. They had virtually nothing to go on. No exact time of disappearance. No exact plan of action. And no guarantee they were looking for anything more than a ghost of imagination from a very ill woman. "Annalise, I don't think it's such a good idea to—"

"I'm going." She crossed her arms over her chest and pinned him with a steely gaze.

He met her stare for stare for all of thirty seconds before he caved. "Fine. You know I'm not letting you go alone."

She grinned, then she spun and marched northeast.

Wilderness, here we come. Ready or not.

He could be so stubborn! And, for the guy who kept encouraging her to trust her instincts, seriously untrusting of them. Every time he looked at her now, did he see father-killer stamped across her forehead? Did he wonder if she'd made the right decision? One of these days—soon—they were going to have to discuss all of it. Even if it hurt. She shuddered. She was not looking forward to that conversation.

Lord, a little courage?

Before she knew it, she and Zach had been hiking a little over an hour since leaving the group. The radios had been quiet and the skies empty now that the helicopter had gone back to refuel and await further instructions, other than the cloud cover racing across the sun, casting them from light to shade and back again. With each new cloud cluster, a not-so-subtle breeze kicked up for a few moments.

Annalise gazed at the forest with love for the richness of her surroundings in her heart. Thousands of fairy wings shimmied on each tree, flashing green and silver and back again, dancing in an unchoreographed rhythm in time to the fickle tease of the wind's breath. She sighed with contentment.

Though she knew the outcome of this case was more than likely bleak, for some reason, this day she felt a surprising sense of buoyancy. For the first time in months, her steps felt sure. Her posture felt strong. Her head felt supremely clear. And it felt good, right, comforting.

A sudden dark cloud rushed to cover the sun, and a strong wind tossed the leaves.

"Um, Annalise?"

"Weather forecast didn't say anything about storms today when I checked."

"Yeah, the sky says differently."

Annalise stopped and grabbed two Frogg Toggs ponchos from her pack. "Here."

He chuckled. "Boy, you really are always prepared, aren't you?"

"I try to be, but—"

"But what?"

A raindrop bounced off her nose. Her thoughts returned to Zach's father. The image of his body reeling backward, eyes glazing over in slow motion, haunted her the most. "Nothing."

"Don't do that. Talk to me."

She took a deep breath and blew it out slowly. "I wasn't prepared to shoot your father."

His footsteps stopped crunching in last year's leaves behind her. "Annalise, don't."

She scooted to a stop. Raindrops began to plink the leaves around them. "I can't help it, Zach. I shot your father. He was a criminal. He tried to hurt us. But he was your father. I'm not sure I'll ever not feel guilty for that."

She expected his comforting touch. Instead, she turned to find him standing rooted to the earth, head hung. What was he thinking? She was afraid to ask.

Rainwater bounced off her head, beginning to pound harder. She slipped her poncho on and moved to Zach, sliding his over his head. When he raised his gaze to meet hers, pain resonated like she hadn't seen since his teenage years. It socked her square in the chest and stole her breath. She was responsible for some of that now. He'd never have the closure he needed with his father.

Tears mixed with the rain now cascading down her cheeks. "I'm so sorry, Zach. Can you ever forgive me?"

"I want to."

"But?"

"I'm scared. Every time I look at you, I wonder what happened that day."

"I told you every detail I could piece back together."

"I know you did. I just wish… I could have been there. Maybe I could have stopped him. Maybe I could have stopped you. Maybe…"

A shudder ripped through her. "If you'd stopped me, Olivia and I would both be dead."

He dropped his head again. "I know."

Would he have preferred that scenario? Her heart dropped through her heels to the soggy ground below and then burrowed six feet and tried to keep tunneling. "Zach, I—"

"We have to keep moving, Lise."

He took the lead, while she tried to catch her breath. Tried to still the thoughts rampaging through her mind. The soft rain, normally a soothing presence as it trickled down the leaves like a lullaby, did nothing to ease the squeezing in her chest.

"You coming?" Zach shouted down the hill with a playful grin.

Nothing within her felt playful. What if they never moved past these feelings they both had right now? What if Zach ended up blaming her, resenting her, for stealing his father? What if she never moved past her own guilt?

So much for the calm surety she'd felt earlier.

Annalise forced her feet to climb forward, to follow Zach farther into the forest. The air grew cooler as the rain continued to fall and the elevation became higher. She shivered and wrapped her arms around her torso, inside the green waterproof layer of safety.

When she looked up an hour later, after slogging through slippery leaves and loose rocks that rolled when she least expected it, she couldn't see a single landmark to indicate their location, and again her heart dropped. She'd zoned out, been blindly at his heels so long, she couldn't be certain of the direction they headed.

The mountaintop they'd ascended led to more mountains, more trees, and no viewpoint far enough to even see a patch of sky. Not that it would matter with the dense cloud cover that didn't seem to be moving on any time soon. Like the mountain peaks had grabbed ahold of the bottoms of the clouds and refused to let go.

"Zach? Are you sure we're still headed the right way? Which direction is Abram's Falls?"

He pointed at the hill behind them and smiled. "Down."

"When was the last time we heard or saw the creek?"

He shrugged. "'Bout forty-five minutes ago."

She glanced upward and tried to gain her bearings, but something felt broken. Her internal compass spun wildly with no sense of that lovely magnetic north. Had she truly been so spaced out that she'd missed the last forty-five minutes of hiking? That wasn't like her at all.

"You okay?"

She plastered on a smile that was a lie, if she'd ever told one. "Yeah, let's keep moving."

"My stomach says it's lunch time. Got anything good in that magic bag of yours?"

Annalise dug for a protein bar and handed it to him. While he chewed, she checked the battery indicator on her handset radio. It was still good, at least. She reached for her compass where she'd stashed it in her back pocket and came up emptyhanded. What? Hadn't she tucked it in her pocket at the falls? She patted her other cargo pants pockets. Nothing. Maybe she'd put it back in her pack?

Annalise knelt and removed her pack. Under the cover of the trees, the large, soft drops reached her but not as many as would have if they were in an open field. Her heart sped as she searched the compartments and found no round, black compass. Where was it?

She'd slipped a couple times on the climb. Maybe it had fallen out? She took a deep breath and blew it out slowly, but it did nothing to calm the rising of her pulse.

She glanced back down the mountain. They could return and hope they stayed on a similar path that led to the creek and eventually back to their compatriots in the forest service. But... there was a body out here somewhere, and her curiosity about the case's circumstances climbed with each passing moment. She still had the radio, so they weren't exactly stranded. They had to keep pressing forward. Surely, they'd find the random building the helicopter team had seen soon. "Ready?"

He nodded.

She resumed the lead this time, eyes forward and head in the game again. They couldn't afford to be lost on this mountain.

Chapter Nine

Sunset came quickly without any gradation or bright colors characteristic of their East Tennessee summers. The gray got grayer and then it was nearly too dark to see the path before him. "Time to set up camp, Lise?"

She nodded and stopped walking.

Zach slid his arms around her shoulders from behind. "What's wrong?"

Her shoulders tensed under his touch. "I think we're lost."

He chuckled.

She didn't.

"You're serious?"

She nodded. "I dropped my compass somewhere, and I have no idea if we're headed in the right direction."

His brow wrinkled. Annalise lost in the woods? Had that ever happened? "Okay, well, we can't do much in the dark. Let's set up the tent and deal with it in the morning. What's for dinner?"

She giggled briefly. "You always know how to make me smile."

He kissed the top of her head. "That's my job." He released her, wiggled his damp-feeling toes, and shrugged off the poncho. It had saved him from being soaked like the rest of the forest, but a hot bath and dry clothes would be amazing. At least the rain had stopped in the last half-hour.

He helped Annalise out of her poncho and backpack. "Tent in here somewhere?"

"Yep. Maybe try to find a hemlock or cedar tree for us? The needles underneath will be better sleeping and protection from the rain."

"Yes, ma'am." He tipped her chin up and looked deep into her eyes. "It's going to be okay, Lise. Promise."

"How can you be so confident? How are you not freaking out? You know how much empty space there is out here. If we are really, honestly lost, well…"

"You still have the radio. Right?"

She nodded.

"Call in and tell them the situation and where you think we may be."

"Okay." She keyed up the radio. "Special Agent Baker to park ranger headquarters. You there, Blu?"

After thirty seconds of silence, she tried again. Zach craned his head, straining to hear any crackle or whisper of hope that someone heard them. Nothing.

Annalise's eyes grew wider. She shook the radio. "Think it's wet?"

"Maybe. Not much is dry right now. Including my undies."

"Ugh. TMI, Zach."

He chuckled. "Oh, come on, we needed a bit of comic relief." He tossed a smile her way.

She half-heartedly returned it. "Help me set up the tent?"

They worked quietly in tandem. There wasn't much else to do, so as soon as it was erect, they crawled inside.

"Not very cozy without some dry clothes, eh?" Annalise frowned.

"I'm here with you. It's perfect." He inflated the two pillows Annalise handed him, then encouraged her to lie next to him. He covered them both with the dry, wool blanket and wrapped his arms around her. "Tomorrow will be better."

"Since when have you had such endless optimism?"

"Since you lost yours."

Annalise's body tensed again. He hugged her closer. "What is it?"

"I don't know."

"I've got you."

She sighed. "I'm not sure I'm cut out for this job. Maybe I've had my glory days."

"Oh, Lise. There's no way you can believe that."

In the intense darkness, he could see nothing, but he felt when her tears started.

"Dear, sweet woman. We would not have solved any of the cases without you. You found Cody. You found Olivia. You figured out," he swallowed hard, "my father was the ringleader." He purposely unclenched his newly-formed fist. "And you are going to help figure this one out too. Like you always do. You're brilliant. And beautiful. And I know you can get through whatever those demons are telling you in there." He tapped her head with his index finger.

"I don't want to fight anymore."

"Fight what?"

"The doubt. The constant, nagging, ugly voice that is torturing me every minute of every day."

Zach sighed. "You can't let what that lousy jerk said about you haunt you forever."

"It isn't just what he said. It's what he did. I wasn't good enough to make him want to stay. A good enough wife. A good enough lover. A good enough anything to succeed at the most important vow I'd ever made. And, now, on top of that, I wasn't a good enough agent to avoid shooting *your father*. How can you even look at me?"

He gently tugged her chin so that she faced him. He clicked on the flashlight. "I love looking at you. You did your best."

"You have no doubts?"

He hesitated. He couldn't lie and tell her he didn't, but he couldn't say he did without pulling her farther into the mud pit. "It's a terrible situation. I wasn't there. I wish I had been. This would be easier if it'd been me and not you."

"You'd have killed your own father?"

"If I had to."

"And that would've been easier?"

"Yes. Then you wouldn't be hurting like you are." He clicked off the flashlight.

Her lips pressed softly against his. "I love you, Zach."

"I love you too, Lise." He snugged her in as close as possible. "Get some sleep. Big day tomorrow."

"What if we really are lost?"

"No one I'd rather be lost with, my dear. We'll just squat, live off-grid, have squirrels marry us, and be happily-ever-after fairy-talers."

She giggled. "Whatever. You'd die without Cracker Barrel."

"Granted, it'd be tough, but I'm sure we can figure out how to make killer squirrel dumplin's… after they perform our ceremony, of course."

"You'd kill the poor things that help us become man and wife?"

"Depends on how hungry I am."

She slapped his arm. "Go to sleep, goofball."

He'd have to fight the angry voices screaming in his heart and mind. Because no matter how much doubt plagued him, he never wanted to let this amazing woman go.

Annalise's eyes had stared into the darkness thick as velvet most of the night, watching as the time crept slowly to dawn. Zach's heavy, warm arm was the only thing that kept the racing thoughts from raising her body and driving her into the pitch-black forest.

When the tent finally began to grow lighter, Annalise didn't, at first, realize the interminable night was over. Suddenly, she could see the stitching in the corners. Faintly, but definitive. Dawn! At last!

She waited until the sun began to sketch the easterly tent side yellow before gently lifting Zach's arm. "Hey, time to get up." For a moment, she pressed her eyes closed again and imagined what it would be like to wake up next to him every morning. On her mind because of their squirrel discussion the night prior? Or because her heart was leading her down that path by itself?

"Morning, beautiful." Zach kissed her cheek. "You didn't sleep much."

"Sorry. I didn't mean to keep you up."

"You didn't. The ground did. I miss my bed."

Annalise chuckled.

"And breakfast."

"Protein bars and water will have to suffice. We've got work to do."

She stretched as she rose. Her clothing still felt damp, but it seemed the sun was shining this morning. *Thank you, Lord.*

Annalise emerged from the cocoon of canvas to a sparkling, brilliant world. The morning sunlight beaming through the canopy in crystal clear air lit each leftover raindrop like diamond tiaras sprinkled on every royal branch.

Zach stepped out behind her. "Gorgeous."

She glanced toward him, but he was boring a hole through her instead of the forest. She blushed. "What?"

"Not a thing. I'll take down the tent while you make breakfast."

She chuckled. "Deal." Annalise sat on a nearby stump and dug two protein bars from her bag. "Done."

"Me too." The tent lay in a tangled heap at Zach's feet.

"Very funny. You know, it has to actually fit back in my pack."

"You skimped on breakfast so…" He shot her a huge grin.

"I'm glad you're in a good mood. We are lost. Food isn't exactly a priority."

He harrumphed. "Always a priority. Besides, we aren't lost."

"How's that?"

"I know exactly where we are." He paused, his grin turning impish. "I'm here, and you're there."

"Ha. Ha. Very funny." She scanned the treetops. "At least we know east is thataway." She pointed. "And west, north, south. So… we should be walking that way, assuming we never veered very far off course, which is a big assumption considering we have been hiking so long and should've already passed the four-mile mark, and we should've found the cabin, and I have no idea where the creek is in relation to where we are now and—"

"Stop. Get out of your head, Annalise Raven."

Ooh, her full first name, and the middle one too. She must really be in trouble here. She put her hands on her hips and glared at him. "Seriously, do you have a plan?"

"Indeed, I do."

"Care to share?"

"We keep moving." He smiled. "Oh, got a bag of rice handy?"

"What? No."

"Okay, the radio is dead, too wet. No rice though, so we figure out how to be on our own. Done it before."

"Time to do it again. You're right." She cleared her throat. "Okay, northeast is that way." She spun. "The creek is approximately that way."

He adjusted her arm slightly to point more to the left.

"Cabin should be that way." She pointed with the opposite hand.

"All right. Let's go." He grabbed one of the bars and ripped it open. "Fast food."

"Clever."

They resumed their hike, in squishy socks but under a clear sky. It took less than an hour for the humidity and temperature to rise to summertime levels, and soon, the rainwater from yesterday would've been a welcome cooling addition.

Annalise stopped and ripped the cap off her water bottle. "Why haven't we gotten there yet?" She took a swig of the tepid water as she glanced over the valley below.

"I don't know."

Fog swirled through the trees decorating the mountainsides, matching the unrest within her. She'd never been lost in the woods before, let alone in the massive Great Smoky Mountains National Park. Surely, when they didn't report in or show up, Blu would send someone to find them. They just had to stay somewhat near where they were supposed to be. "Let's circle back around. We're off mark."

Zach frowned.

"What? Got a better idea?"

His eyebrows shot up. "Nope."

His tone matched her snippy one, but his crawled under her skin and bit her. It took everything in her not to snap a sharp retort right back. Again. Okay, so she had started it. But, still, she didn't like his.

He spun on his heels, and his right foot slipped on the wet leaves. Annalise lurched forward, slipping her arm under his in an effort to catch him. Her feet slid under his, a tangled mess of flailing limbs, and they both hit the ground, hard. His elbow dug into her ribs. "Oof, Zach, get off."

He didn't move. Didn't so much as mumble.

With his entire weight on top of her, she struggled to breathe. "Zach!"

She shoved as hard as she could, and his limp form rolled to the side. "Zach?" What in the world? Had he hit his head? She shook him, as panic crept in and made her heart race. "Zach!"

He moaned.

"Zach, you have to wake up. Please." She lifted the edges of his hair and looked for cuts or bumps. *Lord, I don't understand. Help!*

Annalise's fingers palpated a growing lump on the side of Zach's head. Ah, there. He groaned louder when she pressed on it. "Come on, Zach. Wake up." It couldn't be good after his head injury just a few short weeks ago that he'd gone and done it again.

"Lise?" His eyes fluttered with the single slurred word.

"Right here."

"Who hit me?"

The nervousness erupted from her in a wobbly giggle. "No one. You hit the ground."

"Did I hurt it?"

"I kind of doubt it."

"Shame. It hurt me." He reached for his head.

Annalise helped him sit upright and then huffed down in a heap next to him. "You have a tendency to be incapacitated at the most inopportune moments, Mr. Leebow."

"Not incapacitated." Zach tried to stand and promptly fell back to his rear.

Annalise rolled her eyes. "Right." What were they supposed to do now? They had to keep moving, in one direction or another. She didn't have enough provisions for an entire vacation in the mountains here.

The fear that his last injury had instilled surfaced again. She'd been chasing down the cartel and, yet, what they could do to her hadn't been nearly as terrifying as the idea of losing Zach in that Nashville hospital.

She hoisted Zach to his feet and steadied him for a few moments while he struggled to maintain balance.

He flashed a smile. "See. All good."

"Can you walk?"

He took a wobbly step or two, slammed his palm to the side of his head, and groaned. "Yep. Right as rain."

Yeah, she believed that for two point five seconds or less. But what choice did they have? He was somewhat coherent so that was a good sign, right? There couldn't be any bleeding in that thick skull of his if he was upright and able to keep moving. "Come on, nice and slow."

"Down or up?"

"Down. We're going to retrace and find the creek."

"Good plan. Course I don't remember which way the creek is. Everything's a bit fuzzy."

Lovely. "That way." She pointed down and right. "Hopefully."

It took about five seconds to realize Zach shouldn't be on his feet. She looped his arm over her shoulders and tried to help him. If they could just make it back to a point she recognized, they could camp tonight and—

A low humming sound reached her ears. A four-wheeler? Blu was looking for them! Oh, bless him! "Zach, we have to hurry. Come on." She tugged on his arm, but motivating his legs to move any faster seemed impossible. They dragged slowly across the leaves, as if they were weighted with cinder blocks.

"New plan, Zach. Sit down. Do. Not. Move." She helped him to the ground, his back leaning against a tall hemlock she hoped she would recognize from a distance. "I'll be right back."

He must've felt horrible, because he didn't open his mouth to even try to argue.

"Promise you'll stay put?"

He nodded.

Annalise dropped her pack next to him and sprinted in the direction of the motor sounds. *Please, Lord, don't let me miss him.* She scooted, slid, and ran down the steep mountainside and up the next ruffle in the ridges. At the top, she stopped to listen and stem the racing of her heart and heaving of her lungs.

The hum grew into a dull roar, and below her, an ATV popped into view. The rider, a man in camo, glanced her direction.

Annalise's heart stopped. That wasn't Blu. That wasn't anyone she recognized. What if it was the killer?

She dropped to her stomach in the leaves, but it was too late. He'd seen her, locked gazes, and his face paled. Her pulse galloped back to life as the few seconds stretched into an abyss of time.

He reached for something on his side.

No! Before she could move, he aimed the sleek metal her direction.

Annalise rolled twice, to duck behind the cover of a biceps-sized tree. Not enough protection, but it would have to do. She held her breath and awkwardly drew her own sidearm. She peeked around the tree.

He revved the four-wheeler and raced out of sight over the next dip.

Annalise expelled a massive sigh and leaned her head on her arm, pressing her eyelids closed.

Had she just stared into the eyes of Corinne's murderer?

Chapter Ten

Zach's head throbbed with each beat of his heart. Pulse-slam. Pulse-bam. Pulse-wham. He pressed his palms to his temples, and as long as he kept them there, it eased. But he couldn't walk like that. He couldn't get himself and Annalise back to civilization in this ridiculously helpless state.

He removed one shaky hand and dug through Annalise's pack until he found the first aid kit. He rifled through it, begging it to produce some ibuprofen. Yes! He tore open two packages and swallowed four with Annalise's nearly-empty water bottle. That could be a problem soon. Maybe he should look for some? Her filtered system would stream out any particulates, even if it was puddle water.

Annalise. He missed her. How long had she been gone? It didn't seem to matter lately. Every moment he wasn't with her was a long one. He should look for her, shouldn't he? Hadn't it been a while? He couldn't be sure. Time was one of the fuzzy perimeters escaping his grasp at the moment.

He stood up slowly, wobbly, gripping the tree behind him for support. "Annalise!" His hand flew to his temple. Ugh. Shouting was not smart.

Annalise's face appeared in the forest nearby, followed by the rest of her, like a specter floating in the low, swirling fog. Except beautiful. Not dead.

Boy, his thoughts were super brilliant at the moment.

She held her finger to her lips as she ran closer to him.

He did not like the look on her face, the wide eyes or the frown. "What is it?"

"It wasn't Blu."

"What wasn't?"

"The person on the four-wheeler."

"There was a four-wheeler?"

"You really did hit your head hard, didn't you?"

He nodded and winced.

"We have to get moving. Now."

"Well, who was it?"

"I have no idea."

"Think it was—"

She grimaced. "I'm not sure. But I can still just barely hear the engine. Can you walk?"

"Sure can." He took a few steps that felt steadier than earlier, though still not his normal. "Where we headed?"

"Following the four-wheeler."

"Oh, right." He smiled. "I remember."

The look she flashed him was filled with worry. Probably not the best time to pretend he'd forgotten something, what with genuine forgetfulness hovering so near at such a consistent level.

He trudged through the forest, keeping her back in view as she hurried, then stopped and waited impatiently every so often. The sound of the four-wheeler faded, but he knew she had a directional bearing in mind. Determination stomped into the ground with every step she took. This was the Annalise he knew. Not afraid to follow her instincts. Ready to do what was needed. Where had she been these last few months?

He swallowed hard. She'd been chased into hiding by a jerk of an ex-husband and by Zach. He wasn't proud of it, but he'd been stalking around now for weeks, blaming everyone in his path for the missing father he hadn't had in his life for sixteen years. It was their fault his agent-turned-mob-boss father was dead. It was her fault he'd never have closure. Never get any answers to the thousands of questions he wanted to ask.

How could he explain it all to her without scaring her away? How could he move past it without scaring himself? He didn't want to expose those hard truths and look them dead in the eye. Not any time soon.

He bumped into Annalise's back. Whoa. When had she stopped again? He trailed her gaze. In a clearing up ahead, stood a small cabin. Irregularly shaped brown shingles covered the roof, vines trailed along the exterior walls, and the fringes of the forest pushed in at the sides as if holding it in a woodsy embrace. It belonged there, even though it technically didn't.

"Well, that's interesting, wouldn't you say?"

Annalise nodded. "How do you think he built it without anyone noticing?"

Zach gestured to the trees. "Who's gonna notice?"

"Good point."

"You have a plan here?"

"Not really."

He didn't want to stop her gung-ho attitude, but he had his reserves about marching in alone. "We should get some backup first, don't ya think?"

She huffed. "How exactly? We don't know precisely where we are. Radios are dead. Cells don't work out here. If we leave, while he's in there, we may never see him again."

She had a point. Or he could kill them and no one would ever see them again. "I'm not much good right now either, Lise."

"Right." She puffed again. "Listen, I'll just sneak in for a closer look. The four-wheeler's out front, so he's there. This could be our best chance."

"I don't like it."

"I didn't ask if you did."

The spunky fire she spat at him made him take a step back. "Fine."

"I've got my gun. I'll be fine."

"Shoot first, ask questions later. You're good at that." He instantly regretted saying his thoughts out loud.

A look of hurt crossed her face, followed by deepening of the shadows in her eyes.

He'd messed up. Big time. It was too late to take back now.

Annalise spun and marched through the trees without uttering another sound.

Great. Freudian slips were so not helpful at times like these.

Annalise had to force the tears to stay put. She had work to do. Sneaking up to a murderer's secret cabin in the middle of nowhere with no backup required stealth and concentration. She felt neither. All she felt was the hurt coursing through her, landing in her heart and pummeling it to tiny, broken pieces. Ugly confetti sprinkling all over the forest at her feet.

Zach did blame her.

She knew it all along.

She inched closer to the cabin, where a narrow window looked out over the leaves.

"Stop right there." The barrel of a shotgun slid out of the glassless window along with the deep, ringing words.

Annalise froze.

"One more step, and you will regret it."

She had no doubt of it. "I'm a federal agent. They'll look for me."

"What do you want?"

How did she answer that without provoking him to shoot her? "We're lost."

The man chuckled. "Great agents you are."

"Yes, well, I didn't claim to be great."

"If I tell you how to get back, will you leave me alone?"

Fat chance of that. "You realize you're squatting illegally on federal land, right?"

"Ain't hurting no one. Just want to be left alone."

She snorted. "Look, I'm coming around to the front door. Let's talk."

The gun raised. "Don't move."

She stepped to the right fractionally. There was a sharp thwack, and something hit her boot. Before she knew what was happening, her foot flew out from under her, and her entire body inverted. The tops of the tree flew at her at an alarming rate, even as pain whipped through her leg and into her hip. A short scream escaped her mouth.

The trees stopped approaching and she bounced slowly, dangling like a fish on a line. Too shocked to speak and too painful to move, she waited. For what, she didn't know. Relief. Help. Reality?

"I told you not to move."

The gravelly voice directly behind and below her made her jump.

"Hang on, I'll cut you down."

"Wait!"

With one swift motion, the man severed the rope and she plopped painfully onto her shoulders and neck, barely processing bending her head so she didn't thump straight onto the top of her pounding skull. It took a moment of lying there in a helpless heap for the blood to return to its proper locations.

A calloused hand appeared before her face. "Come on. I'll help you up."

Where was Zach through all this? Annalise glanced around before taking the offered hand.

"He's behind the outhouse."

"Who?"

The man chuckled. "Your partner. Stealthy one, that one is."

"He does have a concussion at the moment. Normally—"

"Don't care. You need to leave."

Leave? Seriously? He was trespassing in a national forest. Did he really think they were just leaving? "I'm Annalise."

"Oliver Tobias."

"Nice to meet you, Oliver."

"No. Oliver Tobias."

"Oliver Tobias. Got it." Annalise evaluated his strong jaw, clear eyes, and direct gaze. This man was in the military. No doubt in her mind. His shoulders were too erect, his posture too sure.

Herself on the other hand... She steadied her feet and followed him toward the front door, stopping short of crossing the threshold. She didn't need to be inside alone with him, even though, moment by moment, she had less suspicion of him being the murderer. But if not a criminal hiding out, why was he here?

"Privacy."

Annalise scrunched her brow. "What?"

"You're wondering why I'm here."

A chill shot up her spine. She nodded slowly.

"Privacy. This was my great-grandfather's property. Before the park was a Park."

"Oh."

"Come on in. I ain't gonna bite."

Zach moved closer in the periphery of her vision, but Oliver Tobias had lowered his weapon as he entered the cabin. In fact, when she glanced into the dark interior, he didn't have it in his hand at all. Still… "I'd feel more comfortable chatting out here."

"Makes perfect sense, but I got somethin' to show ya nonetheless. Come on in."

Annalise weighed her options. Curiosity won. She stepped into the doorway and let her eyes adjust to the lower light. The cabin was tidy, sparse in its decorating but warm, with Indian pattern blankets thrown over the backs of the chairs and couch. An ancient-looking television with dials sat on a slice of stump in the corner. Somehow it made the space homier. The windows, lacking screens or glass, gave the feeling that the forest was part of the cabin itself. She loved it.

"In here." Oliver Tobias waved her to a blanket-covered doorway.

She peeked inside and drew a breath.

"Found her at the falls."

There was no hint of apology in his tone. No malice. No guilt. "Who is she?"

"Dunno. Been like this since I found her. She was wounded. Near-drowned. Managed to get her breathing but ain't managed to get her awake."

Could it be? Annalise stepped closer. It was hard to tell under the puffy eyelids, deep-set dark circles, and tangled hair. The swollen and puffy cheek and lips didn't help either, but the woman certainly held a resemblance to the photos she'd seen of Corinne Porter.

"Mama, I don't wanna swim," Corinne whined.

Mama patted her head, stroking her silky hair. Mama loved her soft, smooth hair. Like velvet, she'd said. "Come now. We must face our fears at one time or another. Better today than tomorrow."

Corinne took two steps forward and teetered at the edge of the greenish water. "No."

"Yes."

But last time, she'd choked on the mud-tasting water. It burned. Why did she have to learn to swim anyway?

Mama smiled down at her. "One toe at a time."

Corinne obeyed, dipping all ten in at once, then letting her feet sink into the mud. Water covered her ankles. Her calves. Her knees. She shivered as it tickled her belly through her swimsuit. She giggled as the bright pink arm floaties pulled her upward, kept her buoyant even if her legs wanted to drop. Mama's hand helped. Grounded her though she was floating. On her back, warm, pressing, comforting. Corinne closed her eyes and soaked in the sunlight warming her face and the cool water cooling her body.

A flash of a second later, the wind making patterns on her eyelids, Mama's hand was gone. She was sinking. Water was grasping her by the shoulders, pulling her hair, refusing to let her go. Dragging her backward, down. Down. Into the cold, dark, oxygen-free zone of rocks and nighttime. She couldn't breathe. Couldn't move. Couldn't see. Was she even there? Corinne thrashed the water, beat it with her arms. Begging it to back away, to let go.

It was no use.

Her lungs pulled at her throat. Open. Breathe! Water seeped into her nose, trickled down her throat. She coughed, releasing the bubbles she desperately needed.

It was no use.

Tears leaked from her eyes. Her mouth slid open. Water poured in. Like a dam bursting, it rushed down her throat.

A face hovered just out of reach. Mama's but not Mama's. No, too masculine. Too mean. She wanted to scream, but her lungs were full of the wrong thing for screaming.

"She's been like this a lot."

Corinne thrashed on the bed, moaning softly. Annalise wanted to reach for her, wanted to pin her down, help her, shake her awake. Something. The look on the poor woman's face, the sheer panic framed by intense pain... Annalise couldn't stand it. "Isn't there something you can do?"

Oliver Tobias stepped closer, stroked Corinne's hair, and sang softly to her.

Sang? A quiet version of "I'll Fly Away" that sent chills down her arms. "That's... beautiful."

He stopped mid-note. Paused for a brief interlude and then resumed.

He'd heard her compliment. What made it so difficult for him to respond? Pride? Bashfulness? This man intrigued her. He'd apparently rescued their victim, kept her alive, calmed her, nourished her somehow. Clearly, he was a gentle creature. What had driven him to this protected-by-traps seclusion?

"War."

The same odd feeling she'd had when Oliver Tobias had read her mind earlier swept over her. Only Zach had ever been able to do so before.

Zach. Where was he?

She paced to the window and peered out. Nothing. At the bedroom door, she spotted his blonde head on the front porch. "In here, Zach."

He staggered in.

Great. This was just the perfect scenario. Two injured people. A hermit with—she counted the seventeen guns lined on hangers in the living room wall—an entire arsenal of weapons. And her. Without a plan. Because as soon as she'd been hung upside down, dropped, and walked in here to find her murder victim alive, all her plans flew out the windows and joined the birds skittering in the sky.

Chapter Eleven

Zach waited on the edge of the living room for more of an explanation. One that actually made sense, maybe. Corinne was alive. Here. In this off-the-grid, rustic cabin, rescued by an Army Veteran turned hermit. Annalise found no red flags with Oliver Tobias' "story," and she was still mad at Zach to boot. His head was splitting open because his brain, apparently, too was mad at him and would like to escape.

Right.

Made perfect sense.

"Annalise, can we talk outside a moment?"

She looked him dead in the eye with a coldness he never remembered seeing directed his way. "No."

How did he respond to that?

Annalise turned her back to him. "Oliver Tobias, we've got to get her to a hospital. You know that, right? That you can't just stay here?"

Oliver Tobias straightened his shoulders and nodded. "It couldn't last forever, I suppose."

"You'll have to accompany us back into town."

He quirked an eyebrow. "Because I'm breaking the law or because you're lost?"

Annalise smiled. "Both."

From his position, Zach caught the interplay between them but couldn't quite categorize it. It pulled, like a string tied to his intestines, uncomfortably but not the same as her interactions with Blu. He pressed a hand against his temple. "Mind telling me how we're gonna get all four of us back to town with one four-wheeler?"

Oliver Tobias grinned. "Be right back."

As soon as he disappeared out the front door, Zach pulled Annalise to face him. "I'm sorry for what I said."

"It's fine."

He could tell by her tone that it wasn't. But they had other things more pressing to worry about. "You have taken an interesting approach with this retired soldier. He has the victim in his cabin, Lise. Don't you find that suspicious?"

"He isn't the murderer... attempted murderer."

"How on earth can you possibly be so sure?"

"You said I needed to start trusting my gut like the old days. That's what I'm doing."

Zach mentally growled. Of course, she would use his words to argue against him. "He could be a psychopath for all we know!"

"He could be."

"Is it the concussion messing with me, or are you really not making any sense today?"

Her slight smile vanished. "I really, for your sake, hope it's the concussion talking."

He'd stepped on her toes again. "Lise, just listen. We are in a terrible predicament here. How do you know he didn't do this to Ms. Porter? How do you know he isn't out there right now preparing to blow us all to smithereens?"

She shrugged. "I don't."

"So what are we doing exactly? Giving him a chance to kill us and just hoping he won't?"

"We're lost. We need his help or, at the very least, his four-wheeler. And if he is the killer… attempted killer… we can't just leave her here alone. Can we? Do you have a better plan?"

"Almost any plan is better than this one!" Why could she not see he was terrified of the outcome here? That he could do nothing to protect her if she wouldn't work with him? She was being unreasonable and stubborn and—

"You are something else today, Zach."

He had a feeling it wasn't meant as a compliment. Not like, oh hey, Zach, you're amazing, really something else. More like, oh hey, Zach, watch your back because any minute now Annalise is liable to chuck a log at the back of your head.

Annalise turned back to Corinne. She began checking the victim's pulse, looking at her pupils, and examining the bruises and cuts and scrapes on Corinne's face.

"This is our chance. Come on." Zach tugged on Annalise's elbow again. "We can take the four-wheeler and bring help back."

She shrugged free. "I won't leave her. Do what you have to do, but I am staying."

"You can't—" He huffed as the room began to spin wildly around him.

"Zach?"

Her voice came to him through a tunnel, a long, dark one. With a coal-loaded train barreling through it and smashing into his head.

"Are you okay?"

He nodded, or at least thought he did. But he wasn't okay. Up was down, right was left. Light was dark. His brain was mutinying. His backside hit the cabin floor, and he slumped against the wall.

Annalise crouched in front of him.

"My head hurts, Annalise."

"I know it does. We're gonna get you to the hospital. Just hold on a bit longer."

"Hospital sounds good."

She chuckled. "You must really be hurting to say that."

"You look scared."

"Nah. I'm fine."

"You're lying."

"Maybe just a smidge."

"How long has GI Joe been gone?"

Annalise glanced at the clock on the wall. "Fifteen minutes or so."

"That's good." But he wasn't sure why. He licked his suddenly desert-dry lips. "How long has GI Joe been gone?"

Annalise frowned. "About fifteen minutes."

"That's good."

Holy smokes, what was wrong with Zach? Annalise's heart alternated between pounding with worry to stopping dead cold with fear. Was his brain bleeding again? She now had two medical priorities on her ill-equipped hands. And where was Oliver Tobias? Seriously. Was Zach right? Had she jumped to trusting the veteran far too soon?

She swiped her clammy hands on her pants legs as she stood. "Just sit still, Zach. No trying to get up."

At the front door, there was no sign of Oliver Tobias anywhere. No movement whatsoever outside, in fact. Come on, where was he? Maybe he was the villain in this story and he'd run as soon as he had the chance.

Maybe he was getting another weapon. Or preparing a strike. Or any number of negative outcomes her whirling brain could create.

Wait? What was that noise?

The front end of an old Humvee shot over a nearby knoll, nearly taking out some saplings and completely crushing any smaller vegetation. Oliver Tobias grinned from the driver's seat and revved the engine even as he was sliding to a stop at the front of the cabin.

Okay then… she had not expected that. Nor the smile that stretched briefly across Oliver Tobias' face. It made her quirk her lips too.

Zach shuffled his feet behind her and leaned against the doorframe, his face pale.

"Let's get you some help."

He didn't respond.

"Zach?"

"I heard you. Just enjoying you talking to me again."

She couldn't help the chuckle that escaped her. She rolled her eyes. Little did he know just how hurt she still was.

And scared. Worried to death, actually. At least Oliver Tobias had returned with helpful tools and not bombs or ax-murdererish things. She had no choice but to trust him and hope he was worthy of it. They had to get Corinne and Zach both to the hospital ASAP, and unless they all grew wings, the Humvee was their best bet. She sighed. "Okay, what's the plan here?"

Oliver Tobias entered the cabin and tossed words over his shoulder she didn't catch. "What?"

Zach leaned against Annalise's side, preventing her from following. But a moment later, Oliver Tobias emerged carrying Corinne, wrapped in a blanket like a huge, swaddled infant. He tucked her gently into the back seat and turned their direction. "You're up next, buddy."

Zach stiffened next to her and a little growl rumbled in his throat.

"Play nice. This is our ticket home," Annalise hissed. She helped him climb into the passenger seat and buckled him in.

"Ready?"

Her stomach in knots, she nodded. "How long is it to town?"

"An hour. Maybe more depending on how slowly these two need me to go."

"Better get started then." *Lord, please help us get there safely, in time, and not murdered.* Everything Zach had warned played on repeat in her mind. Self-doubt, of which she'd had ample supply, wreaked havoc with her earlier bravado. She slid into the back seat and placed Corinne's head in her lap, smoothing the young woman's bangs away from her cool, furrowed brow. What was Corinne dreaming? Could she hear them? Was she aware of her surroundings and her state or floating in blissful liquid light somewhere lost in her own mind?

The lady agent knew her stuff. She'd made some ridiculous mistakes since approaching his cabin, but what could he expect from a civilian? Agent or not, she clearly hadn't been trained for stealth activities. But she had something to her. Some mettle, maybe's all it was he saw. She was a fighter. Determined.

He carefully steered the nearly-shocks-less old Humvee over the well-known ruts and bumps. Though the dirt path was covered in leaves, he knew the way by ingrained memory. His monthly trips to the tiny mom and pop store at the edge of town were usually four-wheeler facilitated. Hopefully, nothing big had fallen on the trail that the Humvee couldn't pass.

"Where was this beast?" Annalise met his gaze in the rearview mirror when he glanced up.

"Hidden."

"I figured as much."

He gave her a crooked grin, but he wasn't about to tell his secrets. If he hurried, he could drop them at the hospital and zip back up here to retrieve his belongings before they forcibly evacuated him or showed up with a bunch of city-slickers to move things for him. He shuddered.

"Where will you go?"

He shrugged his shoulders.

"You know you can't stay here."

"I'm aware." He didn't want to anymore anyway. If Agent Baker and her half-lucid sidekick found him, who knew what might show up next. His brother had some land up Oneida way. Maybe Alexander'd let him erect a cabin or yurt or something on the back forty. Wouldn't be as invisible as this, the family's old home place, but it'd certainly be better than town.

"How's she doing back there?"

"The same. Corinne, by the way. Her name's Corinne."

He nodded. Corinne. A lovely name for a beautiful woman. He cleared his throat. "Good. Glad she's stable." Well sort of. He'd spent a lot of time over the past couple days wishing the beautiful woman would wake up and tell her story. How had she ended up in the basin? Why did she have no shoes? Who was she? He had gone back and forth a million times, vacillating between keeping her at the cabin and racing her into town. But she seemed stable, even if unconscious, and town... people... noise... It was probably a good thing Annalise and Zach had shown up. It gave him no choice but to bring Corinne to the hospital.

"We're going to have questions for you, Oliver Tobias."

"Better ask 'em now, ma'am. I won't be sticking 'round town for long."

"I need to know what happened, every detail."

"I went to the fall to fish and grab some fresh water. But when I got there instead of fish, I saw her floating at the bottom of the pool. Didn't think much about it, just dove in and pulled her up. She was ice cold. Weak, slow pulse. I did a couple rescue breaths, she sputtered out a whole mess of water."

"Why didn't you call 9-1-1?"

He chuckled. "If you ain't noticed, people aren't my favorite. Plus, as you know, there's no cell signal here."

"How did you know she would be okay?"

"I brought her back home, got her warmed up and dried up. All her vitals were fine. I figured she was under, in the cold water, long enough to send her brain comatose. Was hoping she'd wake up before anything bad happened."

"Don't you think that was a bit irresponsible?"

"What would they have done at a hospital any different? I managed to get some broth in her. But, I'll admit, even I was getting right worried she wouldn't come to any time soon."

"She may have internal injuries."

"She may. And I would've brought her in if she hadn't awakened on her own in the next day."

"Why are you hiding out here?"

"Already told you. Privacy." He could tack on all about how people made him feel like he would fly off the handle any minute, how the nightmares didn't plague him out here like back in civilization, or how last time he'd tried living in town he'd nearly drank himself to death. How the cars and fumes and dust triggered flashbacks the likes of which he'd never known were possible.

He caught her intense stare in the rearview and shifted in his seat.

"Did you find anything on her person that we may need?"

"No."

"Have you seen or heard anything suspicious while you've been living here?"

"No."

"How long have you been out here?"

"Six months or so."

"Has she said anything?"

"Only moans. Like she's trapped inside a nightmare she can't wake from. And, believe me, I've tried."

Chapter Twelve

When Oliver Tobias pulled to a stop at the ER doors, she heaved a sigh of relief. Finally! Zach's head lolled toward the window, and he had been like that for many long minutes, despite her efforts to rouse him.

She leapt from the vehicle and rushed through the doors, all semblance of calm leaving her. "Help, please! We need help!"

The small crowd of waiting patients turned and stared.

"Hello?"

The gray-haired nurse at the registration desk jumped into action, lifting the receiver on the nearest phone and calling for someone in the depths of the building. A Nashville hospital and its chaos from a few weeks ago, the events so eerily similar, swam in her mind. She glanced over her shoulder, half expecting to see Zach's father.

Two women emerged from a swinging door with a stretcher.

Annalise held up two fingers.

The women's eyes grew wide, and the gray-headed nurse still at the counter picked up the phone once more.

Annalise led the women outside, where Oliver Tobias waited, shifting from side to side, arms crossed over his chest and a scowl as deep as a canyon on his face. "Corinne first."

Oliver Tobias motioned the nurses to his side. He helped them move Corinne to the stretcher and then stepped back.

"This woman is the victim of a crime. Her room needs to be isolated from visitors until further notice." Annalise waited for their nods. "Corinne Porter, age twenty-six. Drowning victim." Sort of. "We need to confirm that by dental records, DNA, something."

"We'll do our best."

"There's a missing persons case out of Scott County. Here is the officer's name. She will be helpful here."

The nurses nodded as Annalise handed them a card and then rushed Corinne inside. Moments later two more nurses with a second stretcher exited.

Annalise gently opened the door, pressing a hand against Zach's shoulder to keep him from falling to the concrete. "Zach Leebow. Special Agent with SMIF. Age thirty-two. Suffered a concussion and brain bleed about seven weeks ago. Returned to work too soon. Fell yesterday and hit his head. He's been disoriented, slurred speech, and now unresponsive. Hasn't eaten or drank much either in the last forty-eight hours."

"We'll need you to sign forms," the red-haired woman at the head of the stretcher said.

"Of course." She helped transfer Zach to the stretcher and planted a quick kiss on his forehead. "Come on, Zach. Hang in there." She may be furious with him, but she certainly didn't want him dying on her.

Annalise followed them through the doors.

The gray-headed nurse stopped her at the registration desk and handed her a stack of papers. "And who are you, exactly?"

Annalise showed her badge. "It's a long story." And one she needed to relay to Kirk. It would have to wait a bit longer though. Her cell was dead. She rushed through the mountain of paperwork, leaving most of Corinne's blank. When she returned to the front entrance, Oliver Tobias was gone. She shouldn't have been surprised, but she was more than a little concerned. He was involved in this investigation now. How was she supposed to track down a man who didn't like people and knew how to hide out for weeks on end in the mountains with no one the wiser?

Weaving her way through the halls, Annalise found a quieter waiting room and plugged her phone into the wall. When it finally powered on, she had twenty-two texts and five voicemails. Blu, Kirk, Milt, Zach's mother, her mother… pretty much everyone she knew… all worried about her location and whether she was returning in one piece.

The fear and concern they all expressed sank in. Annalise slumped deeper into the chair. She was exhausted, to the bone marrow. No, to the cells inside the bone marrow. How long had she been awake?

She dialed Kirk first.

"Annalise? Is that you? Are you okay? Where are you?"

She chuckled. "It's me. I'm okay. At the hospital."

"What?"

"It's not me. It's Zach. He fell and hit his head."

"Is he okay?"

She swallowed. "No." Tears sprang to her eyes. No. He wasn't okay. And neither was she, really. "I think his brain is bleeding again."

"I'll be right there."

"There's more. We found her."

"You found her?"

"Yes, and she's alive."

Kirk sucked in a breath. "No way."

"She's in a coma of some sort, but she's alive. It's a very interesting story. I'll tell you when you get here."

"On my way now. We have—you know what, never mind. I'll see you soon."

Annalise hung up and texted Blu. Then she called Zach's mother and then her own and reassured them they were no longer lost on the mountain. Lorraine Leebow jumped in her vehicle while on the phone with Annalise, and she would probably beat Kirk to the hospital.

When Milt answered, she didn't even have time to utter a greeting. "Annalise, you nearly gave us all a heart attack. Again."

She smiled. "I'm getting good at that, eh?"

"Too good. What happened?"

"We got lost. You know how easy it is out there."

"Yeah."

"Zach fell and hit his head."

"That's bad."

"Yeah. We ran into a soldier turned hermit hiding out in a cabin. He helped us get back home."

"Wait. What? You're gonna have to say that part again. Maybe a little slower this time."

"Mr. Oliver Tobias Cornwell. Army Veteran. Probably with PTSD, if I'm guessing right. He doesn't like people and he has been squatting on his great-grandfather's property in a little cabin in the middle of nowhere, north of Abram's Falls somewhere." That's all she managed to learn about the man on their drive. He'd proved harder to question than any victim or perpetrator she'd met to date.

"And where is he now?"

"Have no idea, sir."

"You let him go."

"I didn't let him do anything." She had a feeling Oliver Tobias did what Oliver Tobias wanted whenever Oliver Tobias wanted. "The victim was at his cabin. He'd rescued her."

"Wow."

"I know." Her voice hitched. "I'm so tired, Milt."

"I bet you are, kid. I bet you are."

If he only knew. It wasn't just her physical exhaustion. She was tired. Mentally. Emotionally. Spiritually. *Sorry, Lord!* This job was amazing. More than she imagined, in more ways than one. Cody's face floated in her mind's eye, followed by Paul and Orrin, Olivia and her family, Zach's father... so much had happened the last year. Too much.

"Annalise, listen to me."

She tuned back into the conversation in hand.

"You're going to be okay. You need rest and food. Take a break from the case and spend time with Zach. I'm praying he recovers."

"I'll have to ask Kirk when he gets here."

"I'm sure he'll agree. You've been through an awful lot lately."

Did he think her weak? "I need to check on Helene."

"I'll talk to you later. Seriously, get some sleep."

She would love to. As soon as she knew Zach and Corinne were going to be okay.

Her phone jingled as she was preparing to hit send on the call to Helene. "Yes?"

"Is this Agent Baker?"

"Yes."

"Please come back to ER room two. We need to speak to you about Mr. Leebow."

"What's happened?"

The phone went silent.

"Hello?"

The caller had already hung up. Annalise did not like the tone in her voice nor the underlying anxiety and urgency.

She grabbed her cord and ran for the indicated room. Literally sliding to a stop at the door, she grabbed the frame and tried to catch her breath. "I'm here. What's wrong?"

A room full of people dressed in all colors of scrubs turned to her as if they had one reflex center. One pink-topped woman stepped away from Zach's bed and took Annalise by the shoulder. She led her into the hall and in whispered tones said, "He's going to surgery. As suspected, there's a bleed. We have to get it stopped."

The words stole what little breath Annalise had left. "You… know… his history?"

"We have his medical records pulled up."

"How bad—"

"Bad."

Her feet hurt. So badly. She hadn't run barefoot in the woods since she was a child.

Wait. Why was she running through the forest barefoot?

And where was the sun? Hadn't it been light only moments ago? Why was it so very dark?

She stopped moving, her feet pulsating with each breath. Where was she?

Something was coming. Crunching through the leaves. Hurting her. Yelling for her.

He was coming.

Faster.

She had to run. Her feet wouldn't budge. The ropes around them refused to give.

Her feet hurt. So badly.

He was coming.

Run, Corinne! Why can't you run? Move!

Three a.m. Quiet roads. Quiet halls. Quiet hospital. Oliver Tobias rubbed Corinne's quaking shoulder. "Shhh, it's okay, girl. It's okay."

He probably wasn't supposed to be here at this hour. But what no one knew, never hurt them. As long as he didn't stay too long.

Had the doctors found anything out about Corinne's condition? Why wasn't she now awake?

He stared at her smooth skin, the bruises resolving quickly now, her hair, untangled and spread across the pillow, and he smiled. She was beautiful. "Who are you on the inside, Ms. Porter?" Would he get a chance to find out? What if the near drowning had destroyed part of her brain? What if she never woke up because of it? What if his selfishness to keep her at his cabin had been more detrimental than he'd anticipated?

The door creaked behind him, and he jumped. Oh, great. Caught.

He turned slowly and tried to keep the surprise from his features. "Agent Baker."

"Oliver Tobias. What're you doing here?"

"Just thought I'd check on her."

Agent Baker cocked her head sideways, like a cute bird pondering millet or sunflower. "You do have a soft side, eh?"

He blushed and averted his face. "How's she doing?"

"They have checked everything, blood work, urine, MRI, CT scan, x-rays. All of it is normal, except for the fact that she won't wake up."

"Why?"

"They don't know. They think it may have something to do with the trauma itself, like her mind has just shut off."

"Could be the cold and lack of oxygen, right?"

"That's a possibility too."

"I should've—"

He felt a warm hand on his shoulder. He resisted the urge to flinch.

"They said she's physically okay, that her slight delay in medical care probably didn't affect the outcome."

He sighed. "Good."

Agent Baker seated herself in the chair on the opposite side of the bed. The rings under her eyes were more like frisbees. Her shoulders slumped, her ponytail had slipped toward her neckline, and even her hands seemed to lack the energy to do anything but lie open, limply in her lap.

"How's your partner?"

She swallowed. "They won't let me see him yet."

"He hit his head, right?"

"Yes, but he had a subarachnoid hemorrhage just a few weeks ago. He shouldn't have even been back to work yet, but he's so stubborn."

"I wouldn't know anything about that."

The corner of her mouth turned up for a fraction of a second. "His brain was bleeding again. He's in the ICU after a very long surgery."

"Oh."

"They don't know if the damage will be worse this time or if it could lead to a stroke or what."

"He's more than just your partner."

She nodded and swiped an errant tear from her cheek.

"I'd better be going."

If she was surprised, she didn't show it. "Leave me a way to get in touch with you this time. We will have more questions."

He opened his mouth to protest.

"And you'll want to know how Corinne is doing."

He clamped his lips shut. He couldn't argue that point.

Annalise awoke in the waiting room chairs she'd pulled together to make a longer section on which to lie down. Before she opened her eyes, a squirmy feeling like someone was watching her prickled her skin. She peeled open eyelids that weighed a ton each.

Kirk.

Staring at her.

"This is not what I meant by 'get rest,' Agent Baker."

She yawned. "Yes, well, it's about as good as you're gonna get." Ooh, she probably should not take that tone with her superior, friend or not. "Sorry. It's been stressful."

"I understand. How is Zach?"

"Still sedated. They won't let me see him."

"Why didn't you go home and sleep then? I'm sure Millie would've been happy to see you."

"I sent Zach's mom to my home. She needed to sleep in a bed and mine is closer than hers. Both Millie and Buddy are there now."

She and Lorraine had held hands in silent prayer, silent thought, silent hope and dread most of the night. Around three, Annalise had insisted Lorraine go get actual sleep.

"I see."

"I saw Oliver Tobias this morning too. When I went to check on Corinne around 4:30."

"Oh?"

"Yes, I think he will cooperate with us if we have any more questions."

"Annalise, focus on Zach."

She humphed. "It's better I don't. Working and thinking about Corinne's case—they confirmed it's her, by the way—is a good distraction."

He popped his knuckles. "In that case, we need to talk."

"About…"

"There's a body."

It took a moment for comprehension to seep into her completely drained mind.

"We believe it is connected to Corinne."

"Why?"

"It's a woman. No shoes. Similar ligature markings on the ankles. She was found by the team looking for you and Zach."

"What?"

"Yes, not far from Abram's Falls."

"No." Wait. "Ligature marks?"

"Yes, as if she had been tied for a prolonged period."

"Corinne has them too?" How had she not noticed?

"Yes. We believe she was held captive and escaped."

"But that doesn't make sense. Oliver Tobias helped us."

"We didn't say by him."

"Then who?"

"We don't know yet."

"How do you know it wasn't Oliver Tobias?"

"His cabin has been cleared of any forensic evidence tying him to Corinne before she was seen by Helene at the waterfall and subsequently rescued by him."

"No evidence of a crime committed there, you mean?"

"Yes, his cabin and the surrounding fifteen acres encircling it hold no evidence of foul play."

She sighed. "What now?"

"Medical examiner's. If you're up for it."

"Let me let Zach's nurses know. Can we contact Corinne's family yet?"

Kirk frowned. "Let's hold off just a bit longer."

"Why?" She clamped a hand to her mouth. "Sorry."

"No, it's a valid question. Call it a gut feeling?"

"Okay."

"I think it will put Ms. Porter in more danger if the murderer knows she is still alive. And possibly her family too."

"That makes sense." And she should've thought of it already. Zach would tell her to stop beating herself up. She was running on like two hours of sleep in the last seventy-two hours, after all. She should start listening to him… sometimes. Maybe not now since one of the last things he'd told her was that she had no sense, no ability, no instincts… no worth.

"Ready?" Kirk had walked a few feet away and turned toward her expectantly.

She should make her legs move and follow him.

Half an hour later, the medical examiner, Dr. Howard, hovered over the victim's corpse when

Annalise and Kirk walked in, his blue-gloved hand holding a scalpel.

"Doctor." Kirk stopped opposite Dr. Howard.

He looked up and tipped his chin.

"Anything for us yet?"

"Not… not sure just what yet."

"Dr. Howard, that means you've found something interesting." Annalise smiled. "Please, do share."

"You've figured me out quickly, young Padawan."

She chuckled. "One of my gifts, reading people. Really, it's more about learning people." And she was good at it. Once. Perhaps still if she just let herself believe? She had, so far, been correct about Oliver Tobias.

"Look at this."

Annalise drew a cleansing breath and cleared her mind as she began to take in details of the victim. Mid-20s. Thin. Brown hair, similar to Corinne's. Toenails painted but fingernails bare. No jewelry. Simple, down to earth girl, she'd bet. "From the country?"

"We haven't identified her yet, Agent Baker," Dr. Howard answered. "Shall I?"

"Please."

Kirk stepped back and crossed his arms.

Dr. Howard began, "Ligature marks around the ankles and wrists. She was detained for some time. You can tell mother nature has been at work. I suspect the rain has slowed the progression of bugs and animals, but there's no doubt she has been deceased for a week to ten days. There is evidence of sexual assault, and I suspect that may have been the attacker's primary motivation for keeping our victim for a prolonged period of time."

Annalise's heart sank. How awful that this young woman had to suffer so! "Any way to tell how long?"

"No. We've sent fingerprints and dental imprints for identification. Hopefully, we will have results by tomorrow at the latest. That may lead to a missing person's report and give us a better timeline."

"Right."

"Now, to the most interesting part." Dr. Howard gently rolled the victim slightly toward the right and pointed. "She's been branded."

"Branded? Like a cow?"

"Sort of. It's a bit hard to be sure when the branding was applied, due to the decomposition of the body—I suspect from exposure to the elements, like I said, for at least a week. But I also believe it was freeze branded, not fire branded."

Kirk stepped forward for a closer inspection. "What's the difference?"

"Well, you see how the symbol is lighter than the skin surrounding it, kind of like a flat scar?"

Kirk nodded.

"Yes," she said as she leaned in.

"Burns usually heal with texture, or a noticeable scar. Cryotherapy is commonly used to freeze warts, skin cancers, and other minor skin problems using liquid nitrogen."

"But those processes don't leave a scar, do they?"

"Sometimes, yes, but not usually." He pointed to the top edge of the area. "This leads me to believe it was an intentional, literal branding iron. See the design and its intricacy? The difference is that the iron is cooled rather than heated."

"Wow." Raped and branded. Dehumanized. Annalise's throat tightened and prevented further questions, but Dr. Howard read her mind.

"I suspect it was a form of tagging his prey. It told the killer, 'This is my property. This woman belongs to me.'"

She nodded, certain her face was pale.

"The killer most likely has a medical background or, perhaps, a farming background. We will excise this tissue and attempt to make a rendering of the design. However, I'm not sure how successful we'll be. The skin is extremely fragile."

"It's not much to go on, but at least it's something." Kirk cleared his throat. "Thank you." He touched Annalise's elbow and led her through the double doors back into the hallway. "You okay?"

"I need to get back to Corinne."

"To see if she has a similar mark."
"Exactly."

Chapter Thirteen

Annalise's phone rang as soon as she cleared the doorway into the hospital wing where Corinne's room was located. "Hello?"

"Agent Baker, this is Dr. Bivens. We have successfully stopped Mr. Leebow's bleeding. He is going to be brought out of the medically induced coma within the next hour to see how he is faring."

"That's fantastic news. Can I see him yet?"

"As soon as he is awake and we make sure he is stable, we will begin transitioning him from the ICU. He can have visitors once that happens."

"I understand. Thank you." Annalise stopped at the nurse's station. "I need to speak with Corinne Porter's doctor immediately."

The nurse nodded.

"I'll meet him in the room. It's important."

Again, the young nurse with doe eyes nodded.

Annalise entered Corinne's room quietly, gliding to her bedside holding her breath. Hoping for some change. Some gleam that the woman was still in there. Somewhere. *Lord? Are You ever gonna wake her up? We need her side of the story.*

The doctor entered a few moments of loud silence later. "Special Agent?"

"I need to know if she has any unusual marks, specifically a branded tattoo or design of some sort."

His eyebrows lifted. "I have examined her fairly thoroughly, but my focus has been on looking for internal injuries. Without family permission, it would be outside my purview to examine her physical body on such a personal level."

Annalise's shoulders sank. She understood, but she needed to know. Now.

Where had Kirk gone? They'd entered the ER doors together...

She didn't have time for this. Her mind whirred uncontrollably. Lack of sleep. Stress. Fear. A million and one other things. She dialed Mom Porter's number. "Good morning, ma'am. Sorry to bother you so early."

"I'm up at four every morning. You have news?"

Annalise's mouth stopped for a moment. Kirk had told her not to let them know, but this was pertinent. She forged ahead. "Corinne is alive. I'm with her now."

The loudest gasp Annalise'd ever heard sounded through the otherwise silent phone.

She gave Mom Porter time to process her words, while tapping her finger on the bedrail.

"I knew it. I knew my baby girl would come home. Thank you, Jesus!"

"Mrs. Porter, I need your help. There is a victim who wasn't as fortunate as your daughter. We believe it is the same culprit."

"What do you need?"

"Permission to examine your daughter's physical body."

"Why?"

Annalise took a deep breath and exhaled slowly. "I need to know if she has a mark on her back."

"Was she..." Mom Porter hiccupped through tears Annalise suspected were a mix of relief and fear.

Time for honesty that would cut like a knife. "We aren't sure."

"Was the other victim?"

"Yes."

"Oh, my Lord, help my girl." She sniffled. "Where are you?"

"UT."

"I'll be there in two hours."

"Thank you, ma'am." Annalise would deal with Kirk's wrath, if it presented itself, later.

"You should know Corinne is in a coma. The doctors are unsure why."

"She's not been awake at all?"

"No, ma'am."

"Well, okay. She will be."

Oh, to have the faith this woman possessed. In God… and in herself. *I'll work on that, Lord. Help me.*

She had time to run upstairs and check on Zach. She took the steps two at a time and arrived in the hall outside the ICU, panting. What was going on with her? Oh, right. No sleep.

"Zach Leebow. Which room?"

Zinnia, the nurse that had been present when Annalise last checked Zach's status, widened her eyes. "He isn't allowed to have visitors."

"I'm aware. I want to see him."

"You can't."

"Call Dr. Bivens for me. Now please."

What had gotten into her? She sighed. She was just done with this whole situation.

Fifteen minutes later, Dr. Bivens approached with a puzzled look on his face. "Agent Baker?"

"I want to see Zach."

"He is waking up now." He guided her to a side room and shut the door. "There are some problems."

Her heart dropped. "Like what?"

"We believe he may have had a stroke."

The floor dropped out from under her. Her knees buckled, and she sank into a chair. Hard.

"He has left-sided weakness, speech slurring, and memory loss."

Her hand rose to her open mouth and tears instantly poured from her eyes. "No. Not Zach. He's fine. He's… fine."

"Would you still like to see him?"

She shook her head.

"We'll keep you posted."

"Yes. That's good." Annalise rose on shaking knees and somehow made it outside, though the walk down was a blur. She stumbled to a bench and froze there, staring at the sky growing lighter. It should've been a beautiful morning.

It wasn't.

The sky was falling. Crumbling in front of her eyes.

Her phone rang, and she jumped. She fumbled to retrieve it from her pocket. "Yes?"

"Annalise! I'm in the paper." Helene's enthusiasm was evident.

"Oh?"

"Where I saw Corinne is in the paper. They believe me too."

"Wait, how did the paper find out?"

"I called them."

"What? Why?"

"Because I wanted to tell my story. You gave me courage."

"I did?"

"You believed me."

Annalise's shoulders tensed. "Yes, but, Helene, this is an open investigation. You shouldn't have talked to the media without asking one of us first."

"You haven't come to see me." Helene sounded like a whiny, spoiled child.

"I've been busy working this case, Helene."

She grew quieter. "You don't have to be hateful."

"Helene! I am trying to solve a complex case. I don't have time for this!" Annalise clapped a hand to her mouth. Now she'd really done it.

"I understand." Helene's voice shook with tears. "I'm sorry I bothered you."

The line went dead.

"Helene, no—" She didn't mean it. Not one word of it.

Kirk appeared before her, more like an apparition in the glowing sunlight than an actual human presence. "Go home, Annalise. And don't come back until you're thinking clearly."

"What?"

"Mrs. Porter is here. You crossed a line. Go. Home. Now." Kirk turned his back and strode away with firm, intentional steps.

Great. How exactly was she supposed to get home? Her SUV was still in Cades Cove at the Abram's Falls trailhead. She thought anyway.

She called Lorraine and arranged for her to visit Zach while Annalise drove Lorraine's car back home. Annalise didn't tell his mother about his current status. She couldn't. Let the doctors give her the news. Annalise'd had enough revelations for the morning, and it was barely 8 a.m.

There was nothing to go back to. Oliver Tobias tried. Wanted to. But he couldn't. The cabin was off limits. Instead, he turned his vehicle around and aimed toward his brother's.

Thoughts of Corinne tugged at him each mile he drove farther from the hospital. Each minute headed north made him wish he was still south. What was wrong with him? He hadn't wanted anyone in so long he'd about forgotten what it felt like. Why her? This woman with whom he'd never had a conversation... well, a two-sided one. This woman he'd known for less than a week, and known was a loose term in this case. This woman he had no clue about other than that he'd saved her from drowning and he wanted her to be okay more than anything in this world right now.

He'd have to evaluate that point later. He forced himself to focus on the road ahead and the plan he needed in order to stay in the right headspace. He'd need a large canvas tent, a new cache of weapons, a wood burning stove, an axe, a hatchet, a cot... the list went on for at least a mile in the loops of his busy mind. Perhaps he should stop at the old Army surplus store in Caryville and stock up.

Maybe he should consider grabbing a cheap cell phone too. That way he could check in with Agent Annalise and find out about Corinne.

And there he was. Circled right back to Corinne.

He sighed heavily. It wasn't good to be attached to people. Attachments hurt when they were severed. And they were always severed, one way or another. Whether it was car accidents that took them while he was overseas or his own mind that eliminated all possibilities of real human connection until everyone faded away when he came home. He couldn't blame them. He'd practically shoved his friends and family out the door when he'd returned from Iraq. It just hurt too much. It all hurt too much.

Chapter Fourteen

The sun streamed through her front windows. Annalise's eyes fluttered open. From her place on the couch before the hearth, one beam landed squarely on her chest and warmed her heart. She sighed. It was good to be home.

The front door swung in.

"Zach!"

He took a step toward her with his famous ear-splitting grin stretching across his handsome face.

"How did you—"

She scrunched her brow. Why wasn't he running to embrace her?

Her thoughts were fuzzy. Something was wrong. What was it? She tried to withdraw the something, to make it solidify, to make it tell her what it was.

Zach stood rooted to the spot just inside the doorway, brilliant beams encircling him with sparkling yellow light.

"Zach, what's wrong? What's happened?"

He opened his mouth but instead of words, a trail of blood leaked down his chin.

Annalise gasped. She leaned onto her elbow and scrubbed her eyes with her fist. When she blinked, Zach had vanished. The beam of light instead flickering against her empty wooden floor.

She jumped.

Annalise opened her eyes, lying in her bed, the room dark, Millie snuggled next to her, warm and dreaming. She hoped her doggy pal's dreams were more pleasant than hers. Annalise's heart still pounded. She scooched back to the center from her precarious near-edge perch and took a deep breath. Her phone said four a.m. She'd slept a few solid hours at least.

Time to get back to work.

She threw off the covers.

Millie raised her head, yawned, and then plopped her head back onto her paws.

"Sorry, girl. Too much to do to be still." She had to make up with Kirk, they had a body on their hands that needed identifying ASAP, she had three people in facilities she needed to check on, she had a retired soldier to track down that didn't ever want to be found... She sank back onto the bed. She was exhausted before she even could start this day.

"Lord, I'm trying. Trying to follow my instincts, but You saw where that got me yesterday. Trying to be brave, strong, indefatigable. I need help. Major help. Where do I start? What's the next move?"

Zach.

"But I don't want to see him. Not like this."

She was met by silence. She'd been a Christian long enough to know ignoring God's urgings never ended well, but she was going to do it anyway. Call her bullheaded, but she couldn't see him yet. She was angry at a man who might die. What exactly would she say?

So she should check on Helene. Except she was mad at Annalise too.

So was Kirk.

That left Corinne. Perfect. An unconscious woman couldn't get in her head since she couldn't get out of her own head. Right. Exactly.

Annalise dressed slowly, walked the dogs, grabbed some coffee and a bagel, and hit the road for UT Hospital an hour away.

She made it in forty-five minutes, and by the time she got there her heart was again speeding. Zach was just a right turn away from Corinne. One right turn and one flight of stairs. She shook her head. Not yet.

At Corinne's door, Annalise greeted the security officer with a nod and entered to find

Mom Porter occupying a chair near her daughter's side.

"Good morning, Special Agent." Mom Porter held her hand out.

Annalise gripped it and smiled. "How are you both this morning?"

"My girl's going to wake up today."

"I sure hope so, Mrs. Porter."

"She will. I just know it."

Oh, to have this woman's faith!

"Pop Porter doesn't leave the mountain much. He's got too many critters to care for. But he's called me a hundred times since last night. He can't wait to see our baby girl. I'm gonna bring her home with me. You'll see."

"I sure hope so, Mrs. Porter." Annalise released her hand and tucked her fingertips into her pants pockets. "Did you approve the examination?"

"I did."

"Do you know what they found?"

"Yes, ma'am. A burn mark that don't look like a burn."

Annalise's heart skipped. "Can I see?"

Mom Porter nodded. "Above her left hip on her back."

Annalise lifted the sheet and gently rolled Corinne slightly toward her mother. And there it was. A section of skin that looked almost bleached. On Corinne's already creamy skin it was faint, but it was definitely there. What was it though? She leaned in closer.

A flower? More specifically, a tulip, ringed by a thick, symmetric circle. Hmm, interesting.

"What does it mean?"

"I thought you would tell me that," Mrs. Porter replied softly.

"Yes, sorry. Just thinking out loud." She sighed. "I'm not sure yet." But she'd figure it out.

"Momma?" Zach hated the slur at the end of his syllables.

"Yes, son?"

"Where's Annalise?"

"I don't know, baby. I haven't seen her since day before yesterday."

Had he asked her that already? "Momma?"

"Yes, baby?"

"My head hurts."

"I know, son."

He sounded like a teenager. He felt like a child. Helpless, unable to get out of bed. He couldn't even go to the bathroom like a grown man. And where on earth was Annalise? He couldn't remember anything from their stint in the park, but Kirk had filled him in on some of the details.

His head really did hurt. He touched the bandages encircling his skull. When would they come off? When would the itchy stitches be removed? When would his hair grow back? When would he go home?

Ugh. He was stuck. It stunk.

"When can I go home again?"

His mother smiled, sympathy and tears shining in her eyes. "I don't know. You've got a lot of recovering to do."

He tried to lift his legs—both of them—and adjust them under the covers. Only the right one moved easily.

"PT and OT start this afternoon. Once they evaluate you, we will know more. Remember?"

"Sort of." Everything the doctors kept telling him since he woke up yesterday was a blur. It was there and then it wasn't, like waves receding under a moonless sky. Washing in for a brief moment of clarity and then retreating back to black. Too much of it.

"Can you call Annalise again?"

His mother obliged. A few moments later, she placed the phone on her lap. "Went to voicemail again, Zach. I'm sorry."

"Do you think she's okay?"

"I'm sure she's fine. She's a strong, intelligent, very capable woman."

He wasn't so sure. She'd shot his father, after all. And right now he couldn't remember why or how, just that she had. "Tell me about dad."

His mom's face drained of all color. "Now?"

"Yes."

Lorraine cleared her throat. "Okay. Well, you know we met and married quickly. One night at the theaters I saw this man outside and fell in love. He asked me on a date. Two months later, we were married. Three months after that I was pregnant with you."

She took a deep breath. "He worked all the time. He was a young officer, trying to climb his way to the top. It was hard. Things were not right between us for a long time before he walked away. He had changed." She turned to look out the window. "I don't know. Maybe he was never a family man, wasn't ready for the change in his life. But you know the rest, he walked away and never looked back. I never—" She gulped.

"Never what, Mom?"

"Never thought of him as a bad man. He wasn't a bad man. He was noble, honorable. Hard-headed as a mountainside, but I can't understand how the man I married could turn into the man Annalise shot." She clamped a hand to her mouth. "I'm sorry, son, I know that's a sore subject."

"She was doing her job, Mom." He could say it out loud all day long, but, inside, where it counted, he didn't believe it fully himself.

"Yeah, but it still hurts you knowing the woman you love is the one who had to take down your father."

He lowered his voice to a near-whisper. "Yes, it does."

"You have to get past it. You'll lose her if you don't. And she's the best thing that's ever happened to you."

He knew his mom's words held truth. He had to find a way to believe them, to live them. "Tell me again what happened in Memphis?"

"Boy, you are full of inquiries today. Having your head knocked about a couple times shook a bunch of questions loose, eh?"

He chuckled. "I hate this feeling of empty holes in my mind. There's all this space that has memories, but I can't get to them."

"Well, this one's simple. Your father was trying to hurt Olivia and Annalise. Annalise saved both their lives and shot him. He died. End of story."

"Do you really believe he was… was…"

"Your father was the leader of the Juarez Cartel. Somewhere along the line he went crooked, took a hard left, I guess, and made the wrong choices. Annalise solved the problem."

"But do *you* believe he was capable of that?"

"I'm not sure what I believe about Henry Leebow anymore." Her gaze returned to meet his. "I never thought he'd leave us either. Some people are just capable of things we never see coming."

"Agent Zach," a bright-eyed woman in neon green scrubs entered. "I'm Melanie. You're going to hate me in an hour." She wore a broad grin as she spoke and twitched her blue, fake-nailed fingertips in the air.

"What?"

"I'm here for your physical therapy. I'm everyone's favorite and they hate me all at the same time." She patted his shoulder. "Time to work."

"Okay."

"Speech and OT will be by later."

"Speech?" his mother said.

"To help regain function after the stroke."

"Stroke? He's had a stroke?"

"Yes, ma'am. Didn't the doctor tell you?"

"I haven't seen the doctor since I got back."

"Well, yes, we believe so. A complication of the hemorrhaging. He's a lucky man. Most people woulda done keeled over." Her voice increased its twang on this last part.

He'd had a stroke… he was only thirty-two. How was that possible? "Well, let's hurry up. I've got work to do."

Melanie ceased all motion. Her smile faded. "Oh, honey, you ain't going to be doing nothing but working on getting better for a long time."

"A few weeks does seem like a long time."

"No, Agent Zach, a few months."

His heart fluttered, falling like a slip of paper through still air. "What about the case?"

"I'm not sure what case you mean, hon, but it will wait, or someone else will handle it. You got a lot to do before you will be back to yourself."

Back to himself. He wanted that. He just wanted it now. Annalise needed him, and he couldn't let her down.

Chapter Fifteen

Next on the list, make up with Kirk and get back into the SMIF headquarters where Annalise could access file records. She called him on her way, the image of Corinne's ice-brand mark revolving in her mind.

"I'm sorry," she said as soon as he answered. "I disobeyed a direct order, and I know better."

"Yes, you do." He sighed. "But they found a mark and we would've missed it if it wasn't for you, so there's that."

"I know. I think it's really crucial to this case too. The killer branded his victims. We need to figure out why."

"I've contacted a friend of mine at TBI, Jackie. She's a profiler. I sent her all the information we have. She's going to video conference this afternoon and give me her thoughts. I'd like you to be here."

"Yes!" She cleared her throat. "I mean, yes, of course."

"On a different note, you realize Zach will be out for a long time, right? There's no way he will be back on his feet as quickly as last time."

She didn't respond, couldn't really.

"I know it's hard to hear, but we have to think of other options at the moment."

"What? Replace Zach?"

"That's not what I'm saying at all, Annalise. But you can't work alone. It's too dangerous. Look what happened last—"

"Last time. I shot his father. Right?" Her stomach churned.

"Yes, exactly. And we can't put you in danger like that again without some backup. You're one of the best agents we've got."

"You only have three, including you."

"Precisely." He chuckled.

She suppressed a laugh. "Kirk, I won't shoot anyone this time."

"You will if you have to."

"Hopefully, I won't have to."

"We can't take any unnecessary risks."

"I may have an idea. It's a bit outside the box though."

"Outside the box might be exactly what we need right now."

"Oliver Tobias."

"The cabin soldier?"

"Yep. He's military and he's smart. He's already aware of the case."

"We don't have time to train someone, Annalise."

"I have a feeling he doesn't need training."

"A feeling?"

"Yes."

"That's reassuring."

"You had a gut feeling about not telling Corinne's parents."

"Which you completely ignored."

"Yes, I did. And I apologized. Look, get his military records. See if I'm wrong."

"Okay. I'll see what I can do. But no promises."

"I'll be there in half an hour."

"I'll be here. And, Annalise, don't go against an order again."

"I won't." Unless she had to.

Seated at her desk an hour later, with the case file spread across her desk haphazardly, Annalise leaned back and sighed.

She had no idea what the symbol on Corinne meant. She had no idea who the victim in the ME's office was. Kirk was still working to pull Oliver Tobias' records, and he was ignoring Annalise completely. Lovely.

She dialed Helene's room at Haven for Hope. "Hello?"

Helene sounded happy, bubbly even. "Hi, Helene. It's Annalise Baker."

"Hi!" Helene giggled. "Sorry, that was loud."

"How are you?"

"Great. My friend has been talking to me a lot today."

Her friend? A real person or a voice? "That's great."

"Tells the best stories. Brings me the best sweets too."

"That's great, Helene."

A man's low rumbly voice mumbled something in the background.

"Who's that?"

"I already told you, silly. My friend."

Annalise's pulse quickened. "What's your friend's name?"

"I'm leaving this place soon, Annalise. Aren't you happy for me?"

"You've been released?"

Helene giggled. "I'm leaving soon. Talk to you later, Annalise."

"Helene, wait—" The line went dead. Annalise tried to call back, but it only rang and rang. Great. She looked up the number for the front desk and dialed. "Yes, hi, this is Special Agent Baker. I helped Helene James get into your facility. Can you tell me if she's okay?"

"Are you family?"

"No. A friend."

"I'm sorry, we cannot disclose patient information to anyone that isn't on her official form. Are you on that form?"

"Yes?" Annalise swallowed the guilt of the almost-lie.

The woman on the phone cleared her throat. "Let me double check. One moment please."

"No, listen—"

Annoying elevator music filtered through the line. Oh, grrrr. She didn't have time for this nonsense. Who was the man in Helene's room? And why did she have this awful, something-was-twisting-her-guts feeling in the pit of her stomach?

"Ma'am, are you still there?"

"Yes."

"You are not on her list of approved people to discuss medical items. You may visit any patients during visiting hours Monday through Friday."

"You don't understand. I think she's in danger."

"We take our security seriously, Ms. Baker. If you have a concern, you're welcome to come down and discuss it with us." Click.

Kirk swung her office door open. "Call him." And then he disappeared again.

She dialed Oliver Tobias on the way to her SUV. Thank goodness he got a cheap cell phone. "I need your help."

"O…kay."

"You sound so enthusiastic."

"Depends on what it is."

"What is that noise?"

"I'm splitting firewood."

"You went back to the cabin?"

"Nope. New opportunity. Different place. Same privacy. Hopefully."

"Listen, my partner is out of commission for who knows how long. I don't know exactly what is in that military background of yours, but it's enough that my boss is willing, without questions, to bring you in. I need a partner. You up for it?"

"How's Corinne?"

"Same, as far as I know. Her mother is with her."

"Help you catch whoever did this to her?"

"Yes." Annalise entered her SUV, started the engine, and slammed the door while she waited for his response.

"In what capacity?"

Annalise created a title. "Temporary Junior Agent." She'd clear it with Kirk later. Again-ish. It wasn't quite the same as her calling Mom Porter. Right?

"Okay. What do I do?"

"Meet me at Haven for Hope."

"Dunno where that is."

"I'll text you the address."

She was sick of making phone calls and staring at papers and doing nothing.

Her phone dinged with an incoming text. She glanced at it. Kirk had sent a document. At the next opportunity she pulled over and opened it.

The official ME report.

"Cause of death: Strangulation.

Victim Identity: Female, Nora Peyton, age twenty-six.

Time of death: Approximately May 22, 2020.

Substances: Victim's bloodwork returned with high levels of Xanax and morphine.

Other: No defensive wounds. Ligature marks around wrists. Signs of sexual assault, no DNA able to be recovered. Signs of recent malnourishment."

Boy, what depressing reading. Annalise frowned as she pulled back onto the road. Hearing what the TBI profiler had to say later would be interesting. And hopefully enlightening.

But right now, she had to get to Helene.

Oliver Tobias arrived to spot Annalise pacing on the steps under a sign for Haven for Hope. He studied her for a moment before she spotted him. What on earth had possessed her to call him? Granted, he was more than qualified, but what had given her the notion he could be trusted?

She waved at him.

Time to be part of the real world again, it seemed.

The 9 mm at the small of his back comforted him as he climbed out of the Hummer. He nodded to Annalise. She motioned him over. "What's the game plan, Agent Baker?"

"Need to check on the witness for this case. I've got a feeling something's not right."

Oliver Tobias didn't lay much stock in feelings, but he followed Annalise inside nonetheless.

In the ugly lobby, with its threadbare carpet and generic paintings of oceans, Oliver Tobias placed his back to the corner and evaluated the room while Annalise spoke with the receptionist. There weren't any immediate threats, and Oliver Tobias exhaled. One step down. Who knew how many to go before he could return to his mountain—well, Alexander's mountain.

"She what?" Annalise's near-screech filled the small room.

Oliver Tobias moved a few steps closer. "Problem?"

Annalise turned toward him. "Helene left." She spun back to the receptionist. "How can this happen? She was sick. How can she just walk out?"

"She was here voluntarily, ma'am."

"So?"

"So she was free to leave."

"How can that be true? She—"

He put a firm hand to her elbow and lowered his voice. "Come on."

"What? No. I can't just leave. Helene is the only witness who saw Corinne in the water. She could be in danger."

"Trust me."

She opened her mouth. Closed it again. And followed him out the front door. "Oliver Tobias—"

"Come on." He led her around the side of the building to where he'd spotted several employees taking a smoke break on the curb outside. He leaned in close to her ear. "Maybe flashing that fancy badge of yours can get someone talking?"

She smiled. "Ladies and gentleman, I'm Special Agent Baker. I need to ask you some questions."

All five sets of eyes turned her direction, cigarettes poised in midair in various stages of consumption. Oliver Tobias tucked his thumbs into his pockets and waited a few paces behind Annalise.

"Did you see a patient by the name of Helene James leave today?"

Four of them shook their heads. One nodded and raised her hand slightly. "I did. She had a man with her. Seemed happy. All giggly and smiling."

"Can you describe the man for me?"

"Am I gonna get in trouble for this?"

"Not at all. I just need to get in touch with Ms. James."

The woman chewed on her lower lip. "Okay, well, I didn't really see him all that well. He was balding on top, thin, tall. Walked with a limp. That's about it."

"Can you remember what he was wearing?"

"I only saw him from behind. Um, slacks, maybe. White shirt."

"Anything else?"

The woman shook her head and took a long drag of her cigarette.

"Any of you have interaction with Ms. James over the last few days?"

The one man in the group spoke up. "Ma'am, with all due respect, we just cook and clean. We don't interact much with the residents. It's frowned upon."

"Right. Okay, thank you."

Oliver Tobias walked Annalise to her SUV. "Think that's enough for a warrant for security tapes?"

Annalise shook her head. "I doubt it. If Helene left willingly and was happy, chances are she knew the guy."

"Yeah."

"I still can't shake this feeling, though."

Oliver Tobias frowned. "What's next?"

"The ME sent a report for another victim. We need to research her, a Nora Peyton."

There was a second victim? He didn't like the way this was going. Not at all. How had there been a man out in his neck of the woods kidnapping and killing women without him knowing it? Was he slipping that much? Getting so lackadaisical about perimeter security that he hadn't noticed he wasn't the only one out there?

"Come on, OT, let's introduce you to the team lead."

"Oliver Tobias."

"Yeah, was just trying it out."

"I don't like it."

Annalise chuckled. "Okay. Well, let's go then."

"Lead the way." He wanted to help Corinne, but he couldn't wait till this was over and done with. Hadn't he put these days behind him on purpose?

Chapter Sixteen

"We're coming with you." Annalise thrust her fists to her hips and stared hard at Kirk.

"Fine."

She smiled. She wasn't about to miss out on the visit to Nora Peyton's family. They still had three hours before the TBI profiler was set to call. Plenty of time to learn more about Peyton's life.

"Him too?" Kirk pointed at Oliver Tobias, who quietly occupied a corner of the SMIF headquarters' main lobby.

"Yes. Him too."

"Annalise, are you sure you're sure about this?"

"Positive. You trust me, you always have," even when she'd been doubting herself for months, "and for that I am eternally grateful. I think Oliver Tobias is perfect here. Maybe even long term?"

"One step at a time, please."

"Yes, sir."

"Ugh, don't call me sir, Annalise. We're friends. We just happen to work together." He grinned. "Not like you and Zach, of course."

She felt the color drain from her cheeks.

Kirk's eyes grew wider. "Sorry. Bad timing." He cleared his throat. "Have you talked to him today?"

Annalise shook her head.

"He's called my desk, for you, five times. Don't you think it's about time you returned his call?"

"Later. We've got a lot to do with the case, is all."

"You sure that's it?" Kirk gripped her shoulder and peered into her face.

She squirmed.

"He's going to be okay. Zach's way too stubborn to die or be an invalid."

She winced.

"I'm not great at these types of things. Obviously."

"It's fine, Kirk. Just come on. I have questions for Miss Peyton's family."

In the parking lot, she climbed into Oliver Tobias's Hummer, and they followed Kirk to the family's home in Fountain City, a few miles northeast of Knoxville.

"Thanks, by the way," Annalise said.

"No problem. I'm glad to help. Any idea how much longer?"

Annalise giggled. "It's been like two hours, Ollie."

"Oliver Tobias."

"Just trying it out."

"I don't like it."

Annalise laughed. Hard. "I didn't think you would." When she caught her breath, she turned to him. "Want to tell me what was in that military file of yours that made Kirk agree to my plan without question?"

"Nope." A crooked smile tilted one corner of his mouth. "Want to tell me what made you ask me to be your stand-in partner?"

"Nope." She punched his arm. "But I will anyway. I have a feeling about this case."

"There you go with those feelings again."

"You laugh, but don't you ever remember a time when you had to trust your gut?"

More times than he could count. That tingly feeling creeping up his spine had saved his life more times than he could count. He nodded.

"I've had a hard few months, emotionally. My husband traded me in for a younger model."

"Ouch."

"Yeah. And before he walked away, he said some things that really got to me. Got me wondering if I was really the person I think I am."

"Yeah." He knew a little about that himself. Returning home, having seen and done all that he had, it wasn't easy to convince the people in his life he was still the same guy.

Was he really?

Okay, so it wasn't easy to convince himself either.

"Zach has been my best friend since grade school, and he's helping. A lot. But then I shot Zach's father."

"What?"

"Long story. Boils down to his dad wasn't a good man. He was tied up in a case we worked, and I was the unlucky one to take him down. It really shook me even further."

There was a flow of information, and feelings, that seemed to come uncorked in Annalise.

"I play that day over and over in my mind. Could I have done anything differently? You see, things were always rocky between Zach and his dad, since his dad walked out on him and his mom when Zach was fifteen. And now he will never get any closure of any sort. Not to mention, how did Zach's dad end up being the leader of the Juarez Cartel in the first place?" She took a breath. "And then Zach and I crossed into dating territory, where before it was strictly platonic. I mean, this is Zach."

Was she even talking to him anymore? Or was this soliloquy meant to be silent?

"And as much as I love him, I'm wondering if it was such a great idea. Now he's hurt—had a stroke. Can you believe that?—and before he got hurt, when we were lost, he said some awful things. And I can't go down that road again. I'm just now starting to kind of believe in me again. I can't throw all that out and start over. You know?"

She paused as she stared out the passenger side window.

He opened his mouth—

"I need to look inward right now. I haven't recovered yet. Not really." Her voice was much softer now. "Shooting his dad was traumatizing, but I know I had to do it. Him not believing in me is worse. Way worse. I am still broken. And I don't want to be anymore." She swiped a hand across her cheek. "I'm sorry. I don't know why I told you all that."

He swallowed. "It's okay."

"You're a good listener."

"Thanks." She hadn't really given him a choice, had she? He squirmed. "Shouldn't you be talking to Zach about this?"

"Maybe. I'm not ready to see him like this yet."

"I understand." Seeing a loved one after a trauma was a difficult thing to swallow. He'd seen more battle buddies physically injured than he'd wish in a lifetime on his worse enemy. It was the ones who came home with the internal scars that were the worst though. Like him. Damaged. Broken, like Annalise had said. He knew a bit about that one too.

"We seem to be here."

He pulled in behind Kirk's truck and put the Hummer in Park. The stone-sided house directly in front sat quaintly amid a well-tended flower garden. Stone pathways shot from several angles into dense colors of all shades and shapes. Birds danced across the tops of flowers and grasses, bending them momentarily while they chirped short notes into the summer warmth.

A serene haven amid a neighborhood crowded with homes and people. Oliver Tobias drew a deep breath and followed Annalise to the doorstep.

Kirk knocked.

A balding man with a large red moustache swung open the door. "May I help you?"

Kirk and Annalise showed their badges simultaneously, but Kirk took the lead and introduced the team. "We have information about Nora, Mr. Peyton."

Mr. Peyton studied Kirk intently. "She's dead?"

"Can we come in?"

He studied Kirk for a long moment then fully opened the door and walked into the hallway. "I'll get my wife."

Kirk and Annalise sat on the couches in the den, but Oliver Tobias took up his normal post in the corner closest to the door and with the best view of the room.

A few minutes later, Mr. Peyton returned, somehow looking twenty years older than the few minutes before—haggard, his face drawn, his eyes hollow—with a short, thin woman. She had tears in her eyes and a definitive tremble to her hands. They sat across from Kirk and Annalise.

Oliver Tobias admired how Annalise held herself with such poise in the face of delivering such horrible news to this couple.

"Did she suffer?" Mrs. Peyton asked with a quiver.

Oh, ouch. What a tough way to start.

Annalise scooted to the edge of the cushion and took Mrs. Peyton's hand across the coffee table. "I'm sorry your daughter didn't make it. We are investigating her murder, along with the kidnapping and attempted murder of a second victim. We have some questions we were hoping you could help us with."

She spoke with the tenderness of a mother, yet she had no children. Oliver Tobias's already high opinion of this special agent climbed.

"You didn't answer my wife," Mr. Peyton said.

Annalise turned to him without releasing Mrs. Peyton's hand. "Are you sure you want to know details?"

The couple nodded as if one unit.

"Your daughter was found with heavily-sedating medications in her system. We can't be certain what she felt at the time of her death," Kirk said quietly.

Tears instantaneously streaked down Mrs. Peyton's cheeks. "How did she—"

"She was strangled," Annalise whispered.

Mrs. Peyton collapsed into Mr. Peyton's side. He wrapped his arms around his wife and sobs tore through them both.

It was hard to watch. Even for him. He would never understand the guts it took the Army MP officers to do this on a daily basis.

"We can come back another time." Kirk started to rise.

"No." Mrs. Peyton sat up and dried her cheeks with a tissue. "No, you can't. You ask us those questions, and you find the monster who did this to our girl."

The air seemed as heavy as a sandstorm in the room as Annalise and Kirk dove in. Where had Nora lived? Worked? Coworkers? Enemies? Did she have tattoos or piercings? What was her daily routine? Who were her friends?

Oliver Tobias was sure the Peytons had probably already answered all the same questions when their daughter went missing. The past two months, Oliver Tobias learned as he listened to Annalise and Kirk, had to have been excruciating for them.

He let his mind wander. His thoughts went to a brown-haired woman lying helplessly in a hospital bed. He'd tasted those ice-cold lips, and he couldn't forget them. If only she'd been an active participant in those rescue breaths. He groaned mentally. How he longed every minute since then to press his lips to her warm ones and have her return the gesture.

He took a deep breath and asked himself again what he had agreed to.

Annalise took notes hurriedly as Kirk fired off question after question. She glanced at the Peytons from time to time, but they seemed tireless. Justice for their girl clearly had taken priority. And rightly so. They probably suspected the other awful details of the case, even if they hadn't specifically asked.

On the right of her notepad, she created a similarities and differences chart and filled in the details compared with Corinne.

It shouldn't have been a surprise there were so many similars. Both Corinne and Nora had connections with UT, both were brown haired, between the ages of 25 and 30, light skinned, pretty, kind-spirited Christian women who frequently walked around campus and had similar interests. Hiking, youth groups, reading.

In fact, there was only one difference. Nora was still in school and Corinne was a graduate. Was that significant? She had to assume at this point all these details were.

She noted Oliver Tobias' exit half an hour before, but he hadn't returned. "Excuse me for a moment, will you?"

Kirk and the Peytons nodded.

Annalise found him on the front walk, his shoulders tensed and his face somber. "You okay?"

"Just feeling restless, cooped up. You know?"

She smiled. "You truly are an outdoor wild man, aren't you?"

"Nah, not really."

"I'm sorry I dragged you into this and that you're so uncomfortable." But she needed him.

"I'm tougher than I look."

"That's hard to believe."

Oliver Tobias' gaze jerked her direction, and a slow smile spread over his face. "I'm gonna choose to take that as a compliment."

"You should." She had the utmost respect for him. Whether she knew all his accommodations or not. She had a feeling about him. She chuckled.

"What's so funny?"

"Nothing much." She kicked a loose stone with the toe of her boot. "What do you think? Any insights?"

"I think this is gonna get worse before it gets better."

"What do you mean?"

"I think there are more victims."

"Serial killer?"

Oliver Tobias nodded.

A chill shot up her spine. The thought had already entered her mind, but she hadn't given voice to the thought. Putting it out there almost seemed like affecting fate.

"How do we find them?"

"Look at Corinne and Nora. Both in the Abram's Falls area. Near my cab—my grandfather's cabin. Don't you think that if these two are there, that'd be the place to start?"

"You're absolutely right. But how, Oliver Tobias? It's an awful big forest."

"Dogs."

"We don't have enough to get the dogs out."

He grinned.

"What?"

"I know a guy."

She matched his grin. "That does not surprise me at all."

Instead of responding, Oliver Tobias pulled his phone from his pocket and dialed, stepping farther from Annalise as his voice grew quieter.

She badly wished she could hear the conversation, but she knew if she injected herself over what Oliver Tobias thought of as a personal boundary she'd lose his tenuous trust. And she needed that.

He returned several minutes later. Annalise forced her shoulders to relax. "Well?"

"We're all set."

"What do you mean 'all set'?"

"Jarvis will meet us at the trailhead with the dogs tomorrow morning."

Annalise's to-do list spun out of control. Dogs weren't allowed on the trails. She'd have to get permission from Blu and his team. Kirk wouldn't be thrilled with her taking the reins and letting this particular horse run either. Was this a permission or forgiveness situation?

She pictured Corinne's face, her sweet mother, Nora and the Peytons. How many other victims would this man reach? How many families would he destroy if they didn't hurry? She swallowed. How many had he already?

Chapter Seventeen

Annalise wasn't coming to see him.

Zach drew a deep breath and blew it out slowly. He searched the ugly, bent, dark drawers of his mind. Most of them were unreachable. He had only little blips of the hike and the current case. His mom and Kirk had filled him in, but it was all so fuzzy. Had he said or done something to hurt Annalise somehow? Kirk swore she was fine, every time Zach called. So why wasn't she here, at his side, helping him feel better? Aiming those gorgeous eyes his direction and making him feel all warm inside. Telling him she loved him.

He peeled his eyelids open and stared at the drab, white-speckled drop ceiling for several minutes before attempting to move.

When he made it to vertical, his gaze landed on his mother's petite form curled up on the uncomfortable-looking couch in the corner. Had she left his side at all in the last twenty-four hours?

"Your left side is looking stronger every minute, son."

He'd thought she was sound asleep. How had she seen him staring with her eyes closed? "I hope so. I am ready to go home."

"Never could sit still too long."

He smiled. It felt a bit more symmetrical today. That was a positive sign. "Like my dad." The words slid out of his mouth so easily. He wished he could cram them back in. Scoop them right up off his lap and eat them all at once. Pretend like they didn't exist. Like the thought never formed. Like the man hadn't been an evil, deserting criminal. "Sorry, Mom."

"You have nothing to apologize for. We were all fooled by him. But there was a time when he was a good man. And that's how I'm going to choose to think of him."

"He was not a good man." His words were spoken softly, but they banged against the walls like hammers. "He was a coward and a criminal."

"Zach, son, think of him when you were small."

"He lied to us even then, Mom."

Tears sprang to her eyes.

"He wasn't good. Not any part of him."

She rose slowly to her feet and closed the gap between them. Grabbing his hand, she peered deep into his eyes.

The tears shining in hers hurt him more than the ache in his head.

"You are the good part of him. Don't you forget it. Ever." She poked him in the chest with each of the words. Then turned her back on him and walked out of his room without another word.

Annalise hung up after talking with Haven for Hope one more time. It was pointless begging them to share their security videos with her.

She checked her email for the hundredth time. Still no notification from the petition for a warrant she'd submitted. Ugh.

Still twelve hours until time to get the dogs out in the woods with Oliver Tobias.

Corinne still in a coma.

Zach's brain still screwy.

Still banging her head against a wall.

Nothing. Absolutely nothing about this case was working smoothly for her.

She slammed her phone on the desk and winced as she heard a crack. Figured.

Oliver Tobias entered from the dimly lit lobby at their headquarters. "You okay?"

She dropped her head to her arms, crossed atop the desk. "No."

"Talk to me."

"This case is driving me insane. We have two victims, one dead, one in a coma, with a weird mark on their body. He's out there somewhere, possibly near your place. We have a missing schizophrenic that I'm really worried about. This extensive profile helps us in zero ways." She tapped her fingers on a thick stack of stapled papers on her desk.

Kirk's friend had given them a long update, detailed, bordering on boring, earlier in the evening. Annalise knew profiles were supposed to be eye opening, revealing guides toward serial killers. But it felt more like reading a book report than finding a magical compass.

"I've always been a man of actions, not words, myself."

"I am really worried about Helene."

"You have to focus on one thing at a time. Besides, she is a grown woman."

"She's an unwell woman. I feel sort of... responsible for her."

"You can't do that, Annalise. It isn't fair for you."

He sounded like Zach. "I know. I can't help wondering, though, what if it's related?"

Oliver Tobias frowned. "How so?"

"Well, the other day Helene mentioned something about a new friend. Then she disappears with him only a few hours after the story with her name and interview released. Seems a bit too coincidental, doesn't it?"

"I'll give you that one."

"I just feel like this one's going to be the one that never gets solved, you know? And I hate that. Absolutely hate it."

He chuckled. "I can see that."

"It's late, Oliver Tobias. We have a big day tomorrow. It's an awful long drive for you. Why don't you come to my place?"

He raised an eyebrow.

She blushed. "Oh boy, that sounded not how I meant it to. I have an extra room. I hate for you to drive home tonight and then turn around and come right back in the morning."

"Yeah, I don't know."

"Okay, it's a couch. Not a room. An extra couch. But still."

"I guess, I mean…"

"A lumpy couch. It's horribly uncomfortable. There! I said it. Happy?" She let the smile playing at the corners of her mouth shine through.

"Oh, ho. I see how it is. Messing with the new guy, eh?"

His deep laugh melted her stress away. "Come on, partner. I don't bite. Promise."

"All right. Makes more sense than driving that far."

"We can brainstorm over hot chocolate."

"Sold." He winked. "Lead the way."

This was a dream. It had to be. Or a hallucination. Yes, that's what it was. One of her hallucinations. But she'd been taking her medicine. Hadn't she?

Helene tried to bring her hand to her face to rub the sleep from her eyes. Why wouldn't it move?

Where on earth was she? It was so quiet. So very still and eerily quiet. Not like anywhere on earth she frequented, including inside her own mind.

What had happened? A heavy fog blanketed whatever part of her brain was responsible for remembering things like that. Nothing in her body hurt. But nothing wanted to move either.

"You're not my usual type."

Helene jumped. It took every ounce of willpower within her to turn her head toward the voice coming from the dark.

"Red heads aren't my style."

A thin slit of light slid under a doorway. In front of it, a form in a chair. Too dark to distinguish any features.

"Where am I?" Her words slurred together like she was drunk.

"Somewhere safe."

She shivered. Doubtful. "Where's John?"

"Not needed anymore."

What did that mean? "Needed for what?"

The voice didn't answer.

"What do you want from me?"

He snickered. "You'll see."

A tear leaked from the corner of her eye and down her trembling cheek. What had she gotten into? And how could she get out?

Annalise jerked awake to a light touch on her arm. Her eyes flew open, and she stared up into Oliver Tobias's whisker-lined face.

"Hey, didn't mean to scare you. Been calling your name from the doorway for a few minutes."

"What's wrong?" She rubbed the sleep from her eyes.

"Get dressed."

"It's still dark out."

"Exactly."

She quirked a still-sleepy eyebrow. "What's up?"

"Less asking, more dressing."

He about-faced and left before she had another chance to utter anything. "Okay then." What did he have in mind? And why now? Just when she finally was getting some real sleep.

She struggled into her clothes and boots, fighting the urge to dive back under the covers. Warm, sweet bed.

"Hurry up, slow poke!"

"Yeah, yeah. I'm coming. This better be worth dragging me from the first night's rest I've had in like a year."

"You big baby!"

She chuckled. The aroma of freshly brewed coffee drifted into her room. And bacon. Yum. Her stomach growled. Well, at least part of her was awake.

"Okay, what's so important that we're up this early?" Annalise sat at a kitchen stool a few minutes later.

"Surprise."

"Really, Oliver Tobias? I'm tired."

"It'll be good. Besides, we gotta hurry before time to meet Jarvis."

"Fine."

"You're grouchy in the mornings."

She stuck her tongue out. "Not usually." Huh, why was she so sour this morning?

"You should see him. Soon."

"What?"

"Zach."

Oh, that him. Was that her issue? Her heart ached at the thought of Zach lying in his hospital bed. Head broken. Heart probably broken too. Why couldn't she climb over that wall and visit him?

"It's clear how much you love him."

"But he—Never mind. Let's get going."

"Bring your food. You'll need the energy."

Annalise grabbed her plate and followed him out the front door. Her gear bag waited in the back seat. "You've been busy. Do you actually sleep? At all?"

"Not much. Not since I got home."

"Yeah, I imagine it's hard to readjust."

"You have no idea."

Silence filled the Hummer for many long, dark miles, but her mind raced. She shouldn't have been surprised, she supposed, when Oliver Tobias pulled into Haven for Hope's parking lot. She was. "What on earth do you have in mind?"

"Action."

"Oliver Tobias, I'm a federal officer. I can't break in—"

"I'm not." He grinned. "Give me five minutes then come arrest me."

"What?"

"If you happen to see some video surveillance playing on the computer while you're in there, then so be it."

"I don't know…"

"Do you feel Helene is in danger?"

She nodded.

"Do you feel the cases are connected?"

She again nodded.

"Go with your gut."

"You sound like Zach." A twang of regret shot through her abdomen. "And you don't like feelings."

"Following your instincts is different than mushy gushy romancy feelings. The best men and women I've known had that strong sense of guttural instinct. Like you. You have to learn to listen to yourself."

"I'm trying to remember how."

"Stop trying so hard. It's called instinct for a reason, Annalise."

"Yeah."

"You listened to yourself and brought me into the case."

"And now you're getting ready to help me commit a felony."

"Well, there is that." He chuckled.

She joined him. "Go. I'll close my eyes."

Moments later when she opened them, he had vanished. She counted to 500 and followed. Anything she found tonight would be inadmissible in court. Was it worth it? She pressed her eyes closed, took a deep breath and released it. What was her heart telling her?

Yes. Helene needed help.

It would've been helpful for Oliver Tobias to tell her his plan. No doubt the night security at Haven for Hope would be present, as usual. And then there were residents, nurses, and other staff to take into account. Perhaps the best route was the direct one?

Annalise entered the brightly-lit front doors. "Hello, I'm Special Agent Baker." She flashed her badge. "I've received a call there may be a problem here this evening?"

The young man's ruddy cheeks blushed redder. "Not that I'm aware of, ma'am."

"I would feel better if I took a look around."

"No visitors allowed after dark, ma'am."

"Well, maybe you could join me? We wouldn't want anything untoward to happen. And when I receive any tips or threats, I like to investigate them to their fullest before dismissing them. Don't you?"

He glanced around, tucking his thumbs into his belt and then releasing them. "I don't know…"

"It would be terrible if something bad happened while you're on shift. I'm guessing you're new." She paused.

He nodded.

Annalise's heartbeat quickened, the yarn-spinning tasting bitter on her tongue. "Are you aware how desperate the drug problem has gotten in this part of town? Y'all are a prime target with your full pharmacy."

"I can't leave my post, ma'am." He nodded as if playing a conversation out in his head. "But if you'll go down this hall and hang a left and then a right, you'll find the nurses' station and pharmacy. They can help you check and make sure things are accounted for."

"Great. Thanks." Annalise rounded the corner and let out a massive sigh. How had that lame bluff actually worked? A sliver of guilt snaked its way up her spine. She'd lied. *I'm sorry, Lord. Is 'it's for the greater good' a good argument to excuse my behavior here?*

The last thing she wanted was to encounter those nurses and other staff at the desk. She turned left and made her way quickly down a dimly lit hall. Where was Oliver Tobias? She slipped into an open doorway, a supply closet as it turned out, and texted him. At the same moment it read "Sent" on her screen, the overhead began to blare. "Security personnel needed at pharmacy." On repeat. Five times.

Ah, no doubt Oliver Tobias was busy diverting attention. And young, new guy would be looking for her at the pharmacy area.

She pressed her eyes closed. Where was the security room where the monitors would be? It wasn't near the front desk—she'd looked. But this building wasn't that large. And it wouldn't be in the dormitory for the residents—too much liability there. OT's—Oliver Tobias's—plan would've been more effective had they been able to see floor plans before they entered.

Her eyes opened and there, right before her nose, was a layout of the building with a big "You are here" X. *Thank You!*

She traced the path to the video surveillance room then snapped a photo of it on her phone. A couple minutes later, she stood outside the open door, back pressed to the wall, listening to the voices inside spill out into the hall. Only two men, if she gauged correctly. She held her breath and risked a quick peek around the corner.

More. She needed something more to get these guys out of their seats. But what? She shot Oliver Tobias another text and waited to the count of ten. Nothing happened.

"Did you hear something?" one of the men in the room asked.

"Nah. Look." The second one chuckled. "Gloria's sleep walking in her clown mask again."

Clown mask?

"I'll call Bob and let him know. He's probably on lunch," the first voice said. A few seconds of silence sped by. "No answer."

"Maybe he's at the pharmacy thing?"

"Maybe. I'll be right back."

Annalise scrambled to the last doorway and squeezed into the recess in the wall it created. She sucked in her stomach and held her breath, heart hammering against her ribs.

The security officer strolled past, whistling.

She exhaled. Okay, one down, one to go.

A phone rang in the security office. She heard the second officer's voice mumble something.

"Missing officer? What on earth?" he muttered under his breath as he stomped by.

Annalise waited several seconds and then flew silently into their room. It took only a moment to orient herself to the computer and locate the saved video files. She found the one labeled for the date Helene left their facility and played it in fast-forward motion. "Come on, come on." Wait. She paused the video. Rewound fifteen seconds. There. Helene in the hall with a man. He held her elbow and smiled. Annalise snapped a few photos of his image and closed the file.

Done.

Now to get out of there before... voices echoed in the hallway.

Great.

Chapter Eighteen

Annalise thrust her shoulders back and lifted her chin.

The security guards entered and froze.

"Who're you?" the bigger one asked.

"Where were you, huh? Something's happening at the pharmacy and you two are off gallivanting around the building?"

The men exchanged confused glances.

"Did you at least catch the culprit?"

"What culprit? It was all a false alarm."

"False alarm?" Annalise stepped toward them. "False alarm! Well, lot of good it did you to leave your posts then, eh?"

The hulk crossed his arms over his chest. "Who did you say you were again?"

"I didn't."

"I think we'd better call this in," the shorter said.

"Great idea, boys. Go ahead." Annalise sidestepped and motioned toward the phone. Her heart pounded so fast, she wouldn't have been able to count its rate if she tried. "Have at it."

When they moved past her toward the phone, Annalise bolted through the door, down the hallways, and burst out into the muggy night air.

She took only a moment to orient herself and then sprinted to her SUV. *Please let Oliver Tobias be there already.*

As she reached for the handle, a strong hand clamped her left shoulder. She jumped and spun, reaching for the weapon in her belt as she did.

"Easy, tiger. Just me."

"Oliver Tobias, you scared me half to death!"

"How'd it go?"

"No time to talk. Get in."

"Swimmingly, I see."

"Just get in."

He rounded the SUV and hopped in the passenger seat. As soon as his door closed, she raced out of the parking lot. "I got it."

"Great." He lightly punched her arm. "Got what exactly?"

"A clear photo of the man with Helene."

"Perfect."

"Confused the heck out of their security team too. They will be scrambling for hours. I feel bad about that."

"If it leads to finding her, it will be worth it. Right?"

She shrugged. "I hope so." Several silent miles passed. "There's really no point in heading home, is there?"

Oliver Tobias glanced at the clock. "Nah. I'll text Jarvis and tell him we'll be there when he arrives."

"Sounds good." Annalise pulled to the shoulder. "And I'll email this photo to my buddy at the lab." And text Lorraine to check on Zach. She'd not done that in a day and a half, circumventing both Zach and his mom and communicating directly with Dr. Bivens instead. What was wrong with her? The things Zach said in the forest flew back at her, like dodgeballs specifically aimed at her head.

Each word hurt.

Each insinuation ached more deeply.

She could've saved Henry. She could've given Zach a chance at the closure he so deserved.

Yeah, right. If she was Superwoman and could have rounded that wrecked vehicle in time to wrench the gun from Henry's hand before he killed Olivia.

No, she'd done what needed to be done to save an innocent officer, and her friend, and put the bad guy in the ground. Even if it was Zach's father.

"You okay there?"

Annalise ripped her gaze from her phone and shot it toward Oliver Tobias. "I'm fine."

"Late night break-ins make you touchy."

"This wasn't exactly the most brilliant plan I've ever seen. It wasn't even a plan! Just a dump-me-in-there-and-let-me-fend-for-myself-kind-of-thing. What if they'd figured me out? I could be losing my job and my badge right now. What did you even do in there anyway?" Wow. That came out of nowhere.

Oliver Tobias grinned. "Touchy. Very touchy."

Annalise resisted the urge to punch him.

"I rearranged half of the pharmacy to keep them occupied while you got what you got."

"What if I wasn't able? How did you know I would know what to do?"

"Gut feelings and instincts. Remember?"

"Ugh! You are ridiculous."

"Maybe so, but it worked."

"Not—not the way…" Zach and I would've done it. He never would've thrown her in blindly like that…

But it had worked. She had the photo on her phone, and Scott would be performing facial recognition as soon as the lab opened up, hopefully.

He grinned. "I'm not anyone other than me, Annalise Baker. You brought me in on this, and you can take me out of it. Anytime you want. Just say the word."

She sighed. "No, I need your help."

"That's why I'm here."

Annalise pulled onto the interstate and aimed for the Smokies.

They'd start from a totally different location. His territory. His backroads. He knew them like the back of his 9 mm.

Jarvis knew where to come, so he guided Annalise to a side branch off the main—main was stretching it a bit—road. "Kill the engine."

She did as he instructed.

They hadn't spoken much the last many miles. It didn't matter to him. He enjoyed the silence more than trying so hard to make small talk. "Come on."

"Where's the dog guy?"

"He'll be here. Need to stretch my legs." Truth was, the trees called to him. Pulled him from the vehicle like the morning sky pulled the sun upward. How could he have missed this haven, this little plot of heaven, so much in only a couple days? His first step off the muddy "road" into the spongy, needle-soaked forest greeted him with the spicy aroma of pine trees and moss. He closed his eyes and inhaled deeply. This was home.

And he could never live here again.

Would anywhere else in the world speak to him the same way this particular place had? The wind that whispered through the night leaves. The moon that quietly sang to him in the lonely nights. The coyotes yipping, the owls hooting, the crickets chirping, the cicadas buzzing. And the newest addition, Corinne's soft moans as she dreamt in her lost inner world.

Perhaps if Corinne could come, anywhere could be home?

His eyes snapped open. "Annalise?"

"Over here!"

He found her on the other side of the vehicle. "What are you doing?"

"Do you smell something?"

He lifted his nose to the air and sniffed. "No."

"Weird. Okay. What now?"

"We wait."

"Lovely."

"I'll give you a tour."

Annalise wrinkled her brow. "Of what?"

"My backyard." He spread his arms wide, encompassing the basin-like area before them, now lit up in a rosy-golden glow. "My cabin—"

"You mean the government's cabin?" She grinned.

"Funny. But yes, whatever, the government's cabin is on the top of that ridge to the west. This little muddy road was my driveway. One of them. I had a few different routes in and out, depending on which store I wanted to visit or errand I needed to run."

"I didn't think you ever left."

"Not often." As infrequently as possible, in fact. "But a man cannot, in this lovely day and age, get everything he needs from the land."

"Let me ask you something, OT."

"Oliver Tobias." He turned to face her.

She crossed her arms over her chest and tilted her head. "Was this about living off the grid and privacy? Or about living away from all human connection?"

He flared his nostrils. "The second."

Her voice dropped to a near-whisper. "Why? What happened to you?"

"You wouldn't understand."

"Try me."

"I don't want to talk about it. Okay?"

She nodded. "Okay."

How could he explain the way he saw himself now, after the death, the destruction, the things he'd been required to do? How could he explain that he didn't deserve to be loved, to find a real human connection?

She placed her hand on his biceps. "You deserve love. No matter what you've done, Oliver Tobias."

He flinched. She was wrong.

But maybe Corinne...

No. Not anyone. "Do you know if the team searched here originally?"

She pulled a laminated map from her backpack. "Show me exactly where we are."

He pointed out their location.

"No. They stopped here," she indicated the ridge near his cabin and the area to the west, back toward Abram's Falls. "Once we found you, we got tunnel vision, I guess."

"Makes sense, if you think about it. I did have your victim in my cabin."

"True." She smiled. "And you are one suspicious-looking dude."

"Hey!" Apparently, her touchiness moment was over. Good.

The skin on the back of his neck prickled. He spun. "Jarvis! Welcome!"

Annalise flinched and turned.

His friend topped a little hill to the right of the road they drove in on, Seeger at his right side, nose already pressed to the ground. Jarvis waved.

"How did you know he was here?"

"Instinct?"

She rolled her eyes.

Someone sneaking up on him in Iraq would've gotten him killed. "Seeger already got a line on something?"

Jarvis approached and smiled. "It seems so."

Oliver Tobias nodded. "This is Special Agent Baker."

They shook hands.

Annalise let go first. "Thanks for coming, Jarvis."

"It's my pleasure. I love off-the-books, secret missions." He winked.

Seeger whined and pulled at his leash.

"Ready?" Jarvis released the leash to its full ten-foot length.

Annalise nodded.

Oliver Tobias brought up the rear as Annalise followed the pair, winding around ancient trees and up a gradual ridge. It didn't take much exertion for the sweat to start trickling down his back.

And it didn't take Seeger long to stop abruptly. He placed his front paws on a fallen log and whined.

"Good boy," Jarvis praised once he caught up to him. "Y'all are gonna want to see this."

Oliver Tobias stopped twenty-five feet away and let his gaze roam the area, while Annalise closed the gap and peered over the log.

"Another victim." Her voice sounded strained. "I'll radio it in."

They weren't supposed to be out here, looking without SMIF's or the Park's permission. What would Annalise's boss say? Kirk seemed a reasonable man, but Oliver Tobias had picked up on the tension between the two agents.

Jasper pulled Seeger back to hover near Oliver Tobias. "He's still signaling something."

"Could it be this body? Just Seeger all ramped up?"

"Could be. But I can't be sure."

"What do we need to do?"

"I'm going to go back to the vehicles and start fresh."

Oliver Tobias glanced at Annalise. "I can't come."

"Nah, don't need ya."

Jasper was more than capable of protecting himself, but Oliver Tobias still felt torn in two directions. "Holler if you get into any trouble."

Once Jasper disappeared over the last rise, Oliver Tobias approached Annalise. "Same as the other?"

She turned a haunted, wide-eyed gaze his direction and nodded slightly. "She's been here a while. It's just not right. The way this guy dumps them like trash."

Oliver Tobias peeked over the log. Pale, naked flesh, long dark hair... He looked away. Annalise was right. It wasn't right what this guy was doing. But that's how serial killers usually operated, wasn't it? Disgusting shows of blatant disregard for human life.

Chapter Nineteen

"You've made an incredible recovery, Mr. Leebow." Dr. Bivens smiled. "You're young and healthy. This, hopefully, will be a minor setback that you will barely remember in five years."

His mother squeezed his shoulder.

"What about this?" Zach lifted his arms in front of him. The left one didn't rise as high as the right. What they couldn't see was the inside of it shaking like Jell-O in an earthquake.

"In time, with your work ethic and determination, the deficits should resolve."

"And the memory loss?"

Dr. Bivens frowned. "Different matter altogether. That could be from the concussion, and it could be permanent."

"Great."

"Perhaps not. Some patients with head trauma do eventually recover memories of their accidents and both the blips of loss immediately prior to and after the trauma."

He nodded.

"If you'll excuse me, I need to see other patients. The nurse should be in with your discharge papers soon. Keep all your followup appointments and go to OT and PT. I think you'll be surprised how quickly you'll continue to regain normalcy."

"Thanks, doc."

His mom shook Dr. Bivens's hand and smiled. "Thanks." She spun and threw her hands to her hips. "Let's get you dressed."

"I think I can handle this, Mom." He playfully shooed her from the room.

Tying his shoes seemed more complicated than he remembered. His mom entered just as he finished the right.

She bit her lip. "Need help?"

"No." He sighed. "Sorry, no thank you. I have to figure it out." How could it be so hard to do something he'd been doing since he was four? He flipped the laces away. "You know what? They don't need to be tied."

"Zach—"

He held up his palm. "It's fine."

"Still no word from Annalise, huh?"

He growled. "I've called. I've texted. I've emailed. I've bugged Captain Brooks and Kirk. Nothing. No response what. So. Ever."

"I'm sorry, son. She is in the middle of a pretty big case here."

He slumped back against the uncomfortable armchair in the corner of his hospital room. "I know. But still."

"She seems mad."

"Exactly. And I have no idea why. I literally have no recollection of anything surrounding this." He pointed to his head.

"Do you think it has something to do with—"

"My dead father?"

She pressed her lips together.

"And the fact Annalise shot him and I'm mad that he's dead?"

"Are you mad that he's dead or that Annalise shot him?"

"I'm—" He hung his head. He didn't know. Maybe both.

"She was doing her job."

"I know."

"She saved innocent lives, including her own."

"I know." He shrugged. "We've been through this all before, Mom. And, trust me, I've run it through my head a zillion times."

"You have to move through this. You love her."

"I'm trying. Grief has no rules."

"I'm aware."

What did that coldness in her voice mean? "Mom?"

She looked him straight in the eye for the first time since Dr. Bivens left. Her voice dropped to a whisper. "I'm hurting too."

He wanted to smack his own forehead. Of course she was. "Mom…"

"It's fine." She smiled. "Right? Everything's fine."

Except it wasn't. Not really. He nodded.

A nurse entered with a manuscript of papers for him to sign. "Let's get you out of here."

"Best idea I've heard all day."

"I'll pull the car around, son. See you in a minute."

Zach scribbled his name on all the lines and was escorted to the car by the same nurse. He refused the wheelchair. "Headquarters, please, driver," he said as he awkwardly slid into the passenger seat.

"Yes, boss." His mom saluted. "Whatever you say, boss."

Half an hour later Zach strolled—strolled wasn't the right word for his walk post-stroke— limped, dragged, stumbled—something like that—into SMIF's lobby and grinned as Kirk emerged from his office.

Kirk embraced him in a bear hug. "So good to see you up and about, Zach. We were worried."

Zach lifted an eyebrow. "We?"

Kirk blushed. "I was."

"Where is Annalise?"

His grin fell. "In the mountains."

"Oh?"

"She found another body. Eerie-similar to the first victim. We are assuming they are related but won't know for sure until Dr. Howard gets done."

"Right." A dark shadow passed over Kirk's face. "What is it?"

"Annalise is pushing the limits with this one."

"In a good way?"

Kirk shook his head.

Zach studied him. "In a making-the-boss-mad way?"

"Furious." The radio on Kirk's desk crackled to life.

Annalise's staticky voice rang through. "We've got another one, Kirk."

"Let me," Zach said as he followed Kirk to the desk.

Kirk motioned to the radio. "Be my guest."

He lifted the mic. "Photograph but don't touch. You know the drill." Zach waited for her response.

"Zach? How? When?"

"You'd know if you'd answer that phone of yours, beautiful."

"I don't—I—where's Kirk?"

Zach handed the mic to his boss.

"The ME's team is on its way. Hang tight."

"Yes, sir."

Kirk laid the mic down and sat in his chair. "Oh, sure. Now she listens to me."

"Can I…"

"I don't think that's a good idea, Zach. You are literally still wearing your hospital bracelet."

Zach glanced down. He ripped the paper ID free. "Not anymore."

"I know for a fact you aren't cleared to return to work. In fact, your return-to-work date is a question mark at least eight to ten weeks away. I asked the doctor myself this time since someone decided to jump in feet first last time. Or should I say headfirst?"

Oh, ouch. He deserved that. He'd purposely taken the risk of returning to work too early after the first concussion and minor bleed, but he hadn't let anyone know he was going against doctor's orders at the time. "I won't work. I just want to ride along."

Kirk stared at him intently for a long minute. "Fine. But if you so much as blink weird, I'm sending you back and you will not set foot in this office or the mountains or anywhere near this case for three months. Understood?"

"Understood."

Annalise was holding it together. Barely. Every time she closed her eyes, she saw these two women. Their skin mottled with deterioration, blue, black, green.

Every time she took a breath, she inhaled the rancorous odor of decay, even though she was back at the truck. It was like the smell was permanently stuck in her nostrils, clinging to the tiny hairs for dear life like a bat hanging on a cave ceiling. It needed to let go.

Oliver Tobias hadn't spoken since the first victim. When Jasper yelled and Seeger barked his second find, it seemed all the words left him.

His quiet presence, strong, like the oak trees, was all that was grounding her at the moment.

They'd clearly found the epicenter of their serial killer's dumping grounds. All four women, including Corinne, found within a two-mile radius of each other. Did that mean he, too, was here somewhere? Was his home base nearby? What if he was watching everything they did? What if— Annalise shuddered, wrapping her arms around her midsection.

Kirk's Cherokee sloshed through the mud toward them and pulled to a stop a few yards away.

The passenger door flew open.

Who—

Zach stepped out.

Annalise's heart rose in her chest, a bouncing, shiny bubble climbing into her throat. She rushed to him.

He grabbed her in his arms and squeezed.

"You're okay?"

"I will be."

She pulled back and smoothed her shirt with both hands. "Sorry. I, um, I'm glad you're—" How would she finish that sentence? Here? Out of the hospital? Normal? They still had so much to talk about. So many things to resolve. She shouldn't have hugged him like that.

Zach's gaze traveled to Oliver Tobias. "Hey, man."

"What are you doing here, Zach?" Her tone held more spice than she'd intended.

His gaze whipped back to her. He smiled. "Came to see you."

She would not blush. Nope. Her cheeks would not give her away.

"Who's this?" Zach nodded toward Oliver Tobias.

"You remember Oliver Tobias, right? He's my new partner." She winced. She'd forgotten to add temporary.

For a brief moment, he looked like she'd hit him, but he recovered quickly. He shook Oliver Tobias's hand. "Congratulations are in order, I suppose." He flashed her a sideways look, one that said, "We'll talk later."

"Just trying to help out till you can come back, man."

"Keeping her in order, eh?"

Annalise's blood heated. Keeping her in order? Seriously? It was her turn to flash the we'll-talk-later look. And, boy, would they. Even if it meant making him madder than he'd ever been, she needed to set a few things straight. Once and for all.

Chapter Twenty

She gripped the steering wheel tighter as the tires left mud and found asphalt. The time for concentration on driving over, it was time to concentrate on the talk. The talk. The big one. She opened her mouth—

"I don't remember anything, Lise. Not one thing. Kirk said we were lost in the woods. I fell. Something about a cabin, a man…"

"Seriously?"

"Seriously."

"You don't remember meeting Oliver Tobias? Finding his cabin? Finding Corinne? The things you said?"

"No, I'm sorry."

Well, that complicated things. "You shouldn't have come out here today."

"I don't know why you're so mad at me. Don't you get it? I. Don't. Know. Did I do something?"

"Yes."

"What? What was it that was so awful you won't speak to me while I'm dying in my hospital bed?"

"Clearly you weren't dying. You're here."

"Lise, come on." He reached for her free hand. "Talk to me."

She pulled her hand back. "You basically said I'm screwed up and that I screwed up. That I have no good instincts left. That I killed your father and that you believe I could have avoided it."

"I did not."

"You did." Tears stung the corners of her eyes.

"I... I don't know what to say."

"Me either."

"It's hard to apologize for something I don't remember."

"Convenient."

"Maybe you should try it sometime. It's anything but convenient."

Oppressive silence filled the SUV's interior. What now?

"We will get through this." He patted her arm.

"I don't know if I can, Zach."

"But what if—"

"I don't know." He'd never doubted her before, and it hurt. More than she could put into words.

As soon as they reentered cell service, Annalise's phone dinged several times. She pulled over to check her messages.

The first was from Kirk. "Zach is not cleared for duty. Take him home. Also, we need to talk. Now."

The second was from Scott at the lab. "Facial recognition gave us a hit. Check your email."

There were several from Zach. She deleted them all and pulled up her email. "John Prosise."

"What?"

She hadn't meant to say it out loud. "Nothing. I'm taking you home. Kirk's orders."

Zach sighed.

"Prior records include possession, breaking and entering, assault. Current address listed in Pigeon Forge."

Perfect. Her next stop after ridding herself of Zach. Ooh, that sounded harsh. Dropping him off. And peeling out and running away from him until her head was clearer. Right.

Her phone rang. Kirk. "Yes?"

"Straight to the office, please. After you drop Zach at home, of course."

"I have another lead."

"Office. Now."

She'd never heard him speak in that tone before. "Yes, sir."

It took her an hour to take Zach home and circle back to the office. Though she wouldn't exactly say she'd hurried.

Oliver Tobias occupied his new favorite corner in the lobby when she entered. He tipped his head. She mouthed, "Is he mad?"

He nodded and shrugged his shoulders.

Great.

She entered his office.

"Close the door, please."

She did.

"Sit."

She did.

"Annalise, I don't know what's gotten into you."

"Sir?"

"You are a great agent. You have this natural ability. You're good at reading people, at thinking through things analytically, at solving riddles and problems and closing these cases. But you've gone too far with this one."

She shrank into the cushion behind her, hoping it would swallow her whole.

"You cannot just do whatever you please and hope I'll back you." His voice was rising with each word. "I could lose my badge. My career. Everything I've worked for because you don't know how to do your job right anymore."

Ouch.

"Scott called."

"Oh."

"Yeah, oh. How did you get that photo, Annalise?"

"You sure you want to know?"

He held his hand, palm out, toward her. "No. Forget I asked." He took a deep breath. "Listen, I get you've been through a lot. But you've lost yourself and that's turned into losing respect for me."

"I haven't, sir. I swear."

He rose to his feet, hands planted on his desk. "You have!" He took a deep breath. "And I do not appreciate it. You talked me into allowing an untrained man onto our team, you've stolen evidence—and I don't even want to know how you got it—you've ignored direct orders, you've taken off alone on your own agenda. And let outsiders in on a high-profile case."

"Sir—"

"We solve cases. We help people. We do not break laws to do so. We are not renegades. We are not vigilantes. You will follow my orders, to the letter, or you will leave. Do I make myself clear?"

She nodded.

"Tell me your plan. All of it." He sat back down.

Annalise swallowed and finally found her voice. "Helene's missing. You know that."

He nodded.

"I want to track down this John fellow. See if she's there."

"Proceed."

"We will check in with the ME and see if these two victims are in fact tied to the first. If they have the same marking, I want to try to look into that further."

"Good."

"I also want to take Oliver Tobias to see Corinne and check her status."

"Anything else?"

"I've been thinking about the profile your friend gave us. At first, I thought it was useless, but she did say something I think is pertinent."

"Okay."

"This killer is a homebody. Remember? She said he probably works outside the home but doesn't travel far from home because he doesn't like people much and he probably feels most comfortable in places that are familiar. It's familiar territory that gives him the courage to take these women."

"I remember."

"If all his victims were 'dumped' in a two-mile radius, don't you think his home—or at least a building of some sort where he feels comfortable—is probably nearby too?"

"I agree."

"We need another aerial and ground search." She pulled out a map. "Instead of here," she pointed to Oliver Tobias's cabin, "we focus here. Now that we have these three bodies, we can triangulate and be more precise."

"I'll see what I can do. We've spent a lot of money and wasted a lot of man hours on this case already. I can't make any promises."

"I understand."

"Do not, under any circumstance, take off into those mountains again without permission. Deal?"

"I promise." She rose to leave.

"And, Annalise."

"Yes?"

"Don't be too disappointed if you don't find Helene."

"I'll try, sir."

"Kirk." He smiled.

"Kirk." She closed his door behind her. "Ready?"

Oliver Tobias uncrossed his arms. "Where to now?"

"John Prosise's residence."

"Man with Helene?"

"Yep."

"All righty then. Let's go."

John Prosise's house was about what she expected. Dirty. Dilapidated. Dingy. "Circle around back?"

Oliver Tobias nodded.

Annalise knocked on the scratched-up front door and waited. Nothing moved in the late afternoon haze. Not even the wind. "John Prosise!"

No response.

Annalise peered through a cracked window, through a gap in the narrowly slitted blinds hiding behind the glass. Strange. It looked like there was plastic of some sort laid out in the room. Why would there be a sheet of translucent plastic?

She circled to the rear to find Oliver Tobias. "See anything?"

"Nope."

She tried the back door. The handle turned easily, and the door swung open without her even touching it. "That was simple. Mr. Prosise! Are you home?"

Something rancid met her nose as she leaned inside. "Do you smell that?"

Oliver Tobias nodded.

"My imagination or does that smell like something dead?"

"It does."

"I'm calling it in." She dialed and stepped in the house at the same time.

The plastic was there because of all the blood. The blood because of the body. Presumably, John, but it was hard to tell with half his face marred by the gunshot wound.

"Wait here?"

Oliver Tobias nodded.

Annalise carefully made her way through the rest of the two-story home. No more dead people. But no Helene either. As trashy as the house looked on the outside, the inside was surprisingly tidy. No signs of a presence recently besides John. One toothbrush in the bathroom. One coffee cup in the sink. Forensics would have to confirm, but Annalise would bet Helene hadn't been here.

So what happened to her? If she were out there somewhere wandering freely from interest to interest, wouldn't Helene have called her back by now?

The refrigerator held one round black magnet. Nothing pinned to the front under it, but a smudge shone brightly on the polished silver. Hmm.

Annalise stooped to check the gaps between the side of the fridge and the counters. She pulled out a slip of paper. A single phone number. No name. But the letters LC. Possibly initials?

Her phone rang, and she jumped to answer it. "Yes?"

"She's awake."

"What? Who is this?"

"Zinnia from the hospital. It's Corinne. She's awake."

Chapter Twenty-One

Oliver Tobias froze. Rooted in place in the open doorway. Monitors beeped. People buzzed around. Smiles shone on faces. But it was Corinne's radiant beauty that filled the room.

Those eyes. Those beautiful, clear, open eyes. Awake. Studying the nurses and doctors as if she hadn't missed a day of consciousness but still wanted to take in every moment of her return to the world.

He wanted to enter. Wanted to speak to her. Mostly, he wanted to hear her voice. He knew what it would sound like. Lilting, musical, soft and lovely.

Her eyes found him. A broad smile crinkled the corners of her eyes. "Hi."

One little word. And it smacked his world off-kilter. "Hi."

"I know you." She brought her index finger to her chin. "But I don't know how I do."

Annalise approached Corinne's bed. "He saved you from drowning and helped nurse you afterward."

"Ah, yes. It's you."

His heart pounded in his ears.

"Come in. Please." She extended an ivory arm, magnetically pulling him toward her.

Each step was so far, yet so quick at the same time. He stared down into her clear green eyes and smiled.

"Thank you for saving my life."

"It was my pleasure." Love was a strange bird. Happened a whole lot easier than he thought it ever could. A whole lot more surprising and simple on its arrival than he'd been led to believe.

"Let's fix you."

Oh good. Helene had always needed someone to fix her. That's what they'd said anyway. Someone to take the voices and mold them into only one. Someone to replace paranoia with lackadaisy. Someone to truly dig into her ugly—beautiful and unique?—brain and fix it once and for all.

She opened her drunken eyelids that didn't want to cooperate with her commands, and it all flooded back. The dimly lit room, the shackles, the imprisonment. Where was she? Who was this voice she heard but didn't see?

A thin, balding man in a medical mask and gown stepped into view. The scalpel in his left hand reflected light from a yellow-tinted bulb hanging somewhere behind her.

She didn't at first register the pain. Didn't at first feel the hot blood trickling on her skin as he sliced her chest. When it registered, the excruciating sharpness of it stole her breath and made her dizzy. "What are you doing to me?"

"Oh, just a little enhancement. Like I said, you're not exactly my usual style."

How many other victims must he have had in order to have a "usual style?"

The next incision stole the thoughts in her head along with the breath from her chest.

Her captor released a rolling valve on the IV in her arm. She hadn't even noticed its presence until he moved to do so. When had he placed that?

"Go back to sleep now."

Her eyelids fluttered.

"Good girl. It'll be over soon."

Her heart spiked a couple higher beats. This "procedure" or her life?

Sitting next to Corinne's bed, Annalise waited until all the staff left.

"I knew she'd wake up," Corinne's mother beamed. "I just knew my baby girl would return to me."

Corinne smiled and patted her mother's arm. "Love you, Mama."

"I'll see myself out. I expect you two have a lot to talk about." Mom Porter exited the room.

"Do you remember anything, Corinne?"

"Bits and pieces."

"Can you tell me where you were held?"

Corinne pressed her eyes closed. "I remember running through the forest. Knowing he was behind me somewhere. That he would catch me and take me back."

Annalise gripped Corinne's hand. "How did you escape?"

"He had me for a day or two, maybe three—it's hard to tell 'cause he kept me so doped up. But some time in there I realized he left during the days."

Annalise nodded.

"I came out of the drug fog with my one hand a little looser than it had been. I managed to wriggle it free and untie my other hand and feet. I listened hard. When I didn't hear any movement, I crept out the door, up a set of concrete steps, through a one-room little hunting cabin of sorts, and bolted."

"Do you know what direction from the waterfall you came?"

Corinne shook her head.

"Did you see his face?"

"No. He kept it covered. I'd know his voice though. He talked to me. A lot. Told me the things he was going to…" Corinne covered a sob by bringing her hands to her mouth. "I'm sorry."

"Don't be. I can't imagine what you've been through."

"He grabbed me as I was walking home."

"Where?"

"Near Market Square, downtown. And I think he'd been watching me. When he pulled up in the dark van at a stop light, I had this funny feeling. When I was walking home the couple nights before, I'm sure I saw the same van parked in different spots along my route."

That would make sense. Him plotting out the capture so no one could see him and so everything would go smoothly. This man seemed to thrive on the details.

"He wore a surgical mask and gown. Never touched me without gloves."

"A doctor?"

"Perhaps. He certainly looked like one anyway." Corinne yawned.

"I'm sorry. I can finish later. You've just awakened like a miraculous Sleeping Beauty and here I am dragging details from you like that's all that matters. I'm sure your family wants to see you."

"Daddy's on his way. Some people from church too."

"Good. I'll come back in the next day or two and we can finish our talk. If there's anything else you remember before then, please call me."

After dropping the note from John's house at the lab, Annalise finally made it home and crawled into bed. She left her hibernation only to go to the bathroom and let Millie out a time or two. When she finally awoke and felt rested enough to be a human being again, two whole days had passed. Her silenced phone held three voicemails, eighteen texts, and more emails than she cared to count.

She scrolled through the messages while patting Millie's head.

Zach was worried about her.

Kirk too.

Oliver Tobias checking in.

Her mom. Zach's mom.

The ME. He'd finished both autopsies and sent reports. She read over them. Same MO. Same drugs. Victims had been identified as missing young women from Knoxville, both with ties to UT. Same markings. No DNA evidence, though both showed signs of sexual assault.

Cause of death, asphyxiation, same as the first victim. High doses of sedatives in their system.

No doubt about it, their serial killer was precise and consistent. Clean bordering on pristine. Would he ever mess up badly enough they could find the guy?

She threw the covers off, showered, dressed, and ate, all the time mulling the details over and over. She needed to focus on the consistencies. The connection to UT. The markings. The possibility of him staking out campus in a dark van.

When Annalise entered her office, a bouquet of colorful flowers awaited her. *Sorry. I love you. -Zach.*

Kirk knocked on her partially open door. "Good to see you back in the land of the living."

"Yeah, sorry. I hadn't slept in a couple days. Guess I made up for it."

"Understandable. Hey, listen, we've got permission for one more search in the area you requested."

"Fantastic! I'll call Oliver Tobias in."

"He's already here. Been hanging out in your garden the last day. Sleeping on the couch. Can't get rid of the guy." He chuckled.

"Good. When do we head out?"

"Now."

She and Oliver Tobias hit the ground in almost the same spot they'd parked to search with Jasper. This time, though, a dozen vehicles awaited them. Blu waved from the semi-circle huddle he was having with his team. She smiled and returned his wave.

Fifteen park rangers and officers converged and set out on a grid search twenty minutes later. They'd cover as much space as possible while remaining in a line walk, but once they hit crevices or steep mountainsides they'd split off into pairs and search areas marked out by GPS.

The helicopter passed overhead several times as they hiked slowly for an hour, keeping as many fellow searchers in her view as possible. But, finally, the terrain made it impossible. She split off with Oliver Tobias and climbed a ridge. "Feels like we've been going forever."

"That's only 'cause we've had to move so slowly and keep our eyes pinned to the ground. As the crow flies, we've gone less than half a mile."

"That's what I'd estimate too."

Oliver Tobias froze. "Shh, Annalise. Look."

She turned her head toward where he pointed. Her stomach plummeted, even as her heart rate increased. A cabin. A very small, very well-blended cabin surrounded by brush and trees to the point it seemed as if it was part of the landscape. Hiding under a thick canopy of summer leaves, it would've been impossible to see from the air.

Chapter Twenty-Two

Annalise drew her weapon and motioned for Oliver Tobias to follow her. He, of course, already had his 9 mm in hand.

They crept to the cabin, circled it, and knocked on the front door—the only entrance. A padlock secured the door. There was a faint muffled thud from somewhere within. "Good enough for me," she whispered. "See anything we can pry this loose with?"

"Step back."

Annalise did as Oliver Tobias instructed.

He fired one shot into the lock, and it fell from its hinges.

"So much for the element of surprise."

"It was locked from the outside. If there's someone in there, it isn't willingly."

"Good point."

She entered and let her eyes adjust. The one-room cabin held one table and one chair, a lone bulb swinging above it. The kitchenette was lined with open-faced cupboards. Inside, neat rows of vegetables and fruits preserved in clear-glass Ball jars sat unpretentiously. There was not a speck of dust anywhere. Not a single thing appeared out of place, including the single newspaper on the table, perfectly squared to the edges of the wooden top. The natural light filtering through the open front door was the only thing illuminating the space.

Concrete steps plunged into darkness in the middle of the room.

She nodded at Oliver Tobias and crept silently down them. At the bottom she pushed open another door. Darkness as solid as a wall met her. She pulled a flashlight from her bag and shined it into the interior.

Her gaze traveled the length of the stone walls and landed on a single bed. On the very human-shaped lump in the middle of it. She gasped.

"Careful, Annalise," Oliver Tobias cautioned.

The form on the bed moaned.

Annalise moved closer, taking in the IV attached to the person's arm, the fluids dripping slowly from a nearby bag hanging on a tall metal pole. The form under the blanket seemed so limp, breaths barely lifting the covers.

Pain-laced, wide eyes turned and met her gaze.

"Helene…oh, what happened to you?" *Lord, help!* Annalise hurriedly untied Helene's wrists and ankles. "Can you sit up?"

Helene shook her head.

"What happened?"

"Fixed… me…"

"What?"

Helene blinked as tears formed in her eyes. "Home… please."

Annalise's heart wrenched. "Okay, yes, of course. Yes. Just let me get help." She stepped away, and Helene reached for her hand.

"Please."

"Stay here. I'll go." Oliver Tobias took the stairs two at a time.

Men's voices floated down into the room. Blu, if she wasn't mistaken. The gunshot had probably brought them all running. Good.

Oliver Tobias returned. "They sent two back to the vehicles to get the backboard. We will have to carry her to the vehicles and drive to a helo zone. It's too dense up here."

"Makes sense. But…"

He glanced toward Helene. "I know. We just have to try to be patient."

"We have to find this guy," she hissed through clenched teeth.

"We will. They'll go over this place with a fine-toothed comb, and they will find something incriminating."

She nodded. Oliver Tobias was right. He had to be. The guy couldn't be so perfect and so mysterious that they'd never find him. Right?

Zach knelt in the grass in front of his father's gravestone. His mother had suggested visiting might help. Zach wasn't so sure. He didn't really feel much of anything, now that he was here. He'd expected anger or sadness. Something.

All he found was emptiness.

He plopped onto his backside. "All right. Let's do this. I am mad at you for dying."

A trickle of heat wandered through him, as if letting the words out of his head made them manifest. "You left me as a teenager. You left me as a man. You left. You were never there!" And Zach had needed him. So many times. For advice. For football. For girls. For work. For life. "I hate you, and I don't think I'll ever forgive you."

I know, Lord. Forgiveness is imperative. Whether he deserves it or not. But I don't want to.

Was that true? Was his unforgiveness a want? Something he controlled. Something he could choose? Something he could let go of…

A bird landed in the tree whose branches stretched over this particular corner of the huge graveyard. It fluffed its blue feathers and let out a few beautiful notes.

Zach drew a deep breath and blew it out all at once. "I hurt Annalise, Dad. Because of you. Because of how angry I am. I don't know how to fix it. I don't know if she'll… forgive…"

Huh. Interesting.

"I don't even remember what I said." And his father didn't remember anything.

Did it matter the root of the hurt? He knew the biblical answer. Forgive. Seventy times seven. Without asking. Without borders.

"Why didn't you love me? Why wasn't I enough to make you stay?" He'd asked the same questions many times through the years but never aloud.

Let go.

Just let go?

Let go.

Let. Go.

Zach squeezed his eyes shut, drew in another, slower breath. The sounds around him—the breeze riffling leaves, the little blue bird singing for a mate, the utter stillness of the rest of the world—filtered through him. Pressing a calmness into each cell. A clarity that came with each burst of summer wind blowing over him.

I'm angry. I'm hurt. I'm scared of what it means that my father was a murderer, a drug boss, a complete and total failure as a father and husband, Lord. But mostly I'm just sad. Sad that

I never had him to watch my games, to fix a car in the garage, to offer me advice, to be present in my life.

I've always been there, son.

Zach broke. He let go. Of the pain in each tear that started to fall. Each one pulled a drop of fear and hate and sadness from inside him, releasing it to soak into the ground and be gone. Forever?

The hurt will still be there, won't it, God?

Yes.

You'll help me though.

Yes.

He opened his eyes and dried his face. There were still so many unresolved issues and feelings, but the anger had melted like an ice cube on a hot sidewalk.

"I need to slide my arms under you, Helene," Annalise said. "Okay?"

Helene nodded.

"Oliver Tobias will get your legs. Okay?"

Helene frowned but nodded.

Annalise gently tucked her arms under Helene's shoulders and midsection. Her palms brushed bare skin on the left and a thick bandage on the right. "What happened to you?"

Tears shimmered in Helene's eyes under the glow of the rescue team's headlamps and flashlights illuminating the small space and casting eerie shadows in the corners.

"It's okay. You don't have to speak." Annalise sighed. "Ready?"

Helene nodded.

"One, two, three."

She and Oliver Tobias lifted Helene, blanket and all, onto the backboard Blu and one of his team members held. She checked Helene's arm where the IV catheter clung to a now-capped tube. It still looked good, as far as she could tell. Thank goodness Oliver Tobias had known how to deal with it. Annalise tucked the blanket tight around Helene's gaunt frame and tightened the straps over her. "There. Snug as a bug in a rug."

"Don't leave me," Helene pleaded.

"I won't. I'm gonna be right here the whole time."

"Do you smell that?" Oliver Tobias asked.

Annalise lifted her nose and sniffed. "Gas."

"Everyone out!" Oliver Tobias yelled.

The men carrying Helene's stretcher shuffled to the stairs. Annalise released her hand and followed them, with Oliver Tobias on her heels.

A series of clicks sounded behind them.

"Go! Go! Go!" Oliver Tobias pushed his hands against Annalise's lower back.

She glanced over her shoulder as she crested the stairs. The orange flash of igniting fire lit the dark room they'd just exited and flowed out of the door. "Run!"

But they all were already running. They streamed out the door, stopped, and turned as one unit to watch the flames lick the front of the cabin. A sound much like the roar of a jet engine starting to build pressure reached them. In a matter of minutes, the entire cabin was engulfed in flames.

They watched helplessly as the roof caved in and little tongues of fire pierced the cracks between the heavy logs.

She leaned toward Oliver Tobias. "What was it you said about evidence?"

His stony-eyed stare didn't leave the burning cabin.

There wasn't anything to be said.

"Come on, guys. Let's get Helene to the hospital. Oliver Tobias, stay here and see what happens with the cabin?"

He nodded.

White smoke floated lazily from the remaining frame. It smelled like a campfire. Woodsy, aromatic. Too bad it was destroying the serial killer's trail. Which was exactly his plan, Annalise was sure.

She walked beside Helene, whose hand once again tightly clung to Annalise's. As they hiked, adrenaline faded fast. Annalise's legs grew heavier with each step. Her imagination took her back to the basement and drew images of what Helene must've gone through the past days. Annalise wanted to embrace her and tell her it would be okay, but, truth was, she didn't know it would be. He was still out there somewhere.

How frightening that thought must be to Helene and Corinne. She had to find him, to stop him. There had to be a way even without anything from the cabin.

An hour and a half later, Helene lay in a hospital bed, a new IV in her arm and pain medication flowing in. The bandages, the doctor had told Annalise privately, were covering incisions and the fact that the killer had performed breast enhancement surgery.

Annalise was still tossing that information around and around her mind when Helene opened her eyes. "Hi."

"Hi. Where am I?"

"You're safe. Remember?"

Helene nodded. "I was dreaming about him."

"I'm sorry. That must be awful."

"Yeah."

"They're restarting all your normal meds soon, Helene."

"That's good. I feel weird."

"I bet."

"Why did he take me, Annalise?" Helene swallowed as tears slid down her face. "He said I wasn't his 'type,' yet he took me anyway. Why?"

"I don't know. Could be because he knew you were involved and wanted to make sure you didn't talk to the papers again."

"I am such an idiot."

Annalise rose and took Helene's hand in both of hers. "You are not. It was a mistake to tell the paper what happened, but that does not make you an idiot. It makes you a human."

Helene snorted. "Yeah, right."

"I make mistakes every single day. Believe me."

"You?"

Annalise told her about Kirk and how angry he was. About Zach and how hurt he was. About her ex-husband. When she finished, it was as if a weight had been lifted from her shoulders. "Sorry. I didn't mean to dump all that on you."

"Thank you for trusting me."

"We're friends, right?" Annalise smiled.

"It's been so long since I've had a real friend. I don't remember what it's like."

Annalise squeezed her hand. "It's like this."

Helene's grin lit up her entire face.

"I'm sorry I didn't keep you safe."

"This is not your fault, Annalise. I trusted that man, John. I shouldn't have. I've always done that. Trust the wrong people. Get myself into stupid situations." She chuckled mirthlessly. "This time, well, this time it was a bit worse than usual."

"I can't imagine…"

"You don't want to know, but you need to in order to solve the case. Don't you?"

Annalise nodded. "Every detail you can remember. When you're ready."

"John visited me at Haven for Hope. Said he'd seen my photo in the paper and thought I was the 'most beautiful woman he'd ever laid eyes on.' Stupid me, I fell for it. It just felt so good to have someone look at me like that. He was a good actor." She drew a deep breath. "The day I left Haven for Hope with him, he took me to the middle of nowhere. The last thing I remember is a needle in my neck and thinking, 'He's going to date rape me and leave me for dead.'"

"I'm so sorry, Helene."

"I woke up in a pitch-black room. Cold. Confused. Tied to the bed. There was this man talking to me. I asked him about John. He said he was no longer needed. I knew that meant he'd killed him. What did that mean for me? Probably dead too whenever this freak finished up with me."

Annalise bit her cheek to keep the thoughts clamped inside.

"Time got all bungled up in there, between whatever the drugs was and the dark. I never did see his face, you know? He was so careful."

"That fits the others."

"Others? You mean the woman I saw?"

"And three more."

"Were they... Did he...?"

"All four of them were dark-haired, a bit heavier than you."

"Suppose that's why he…" She gestured to her chest.

"I mean, according to the profile we got, this man has a very specific agenda. Now that we have a group of victims, I can say without a doubt he had a type, and you didn't quite match up with his image. Perhaps he was trying to make you fit that image before he… finished his plan."

"Finished? You mean raped?"

Annalise nodded.

"Those poor women."

"I didn't expect you in that cabin, you know."

"Why?"

"I hadn't put the pieces together that your disappearance and the serial killer were related cases. It crossed my mind, but I didn't take it seriously."

"Oh."

"It gives me something more to add to the file. Something more to go on."

"That's good?"

"It's not good that you had to go through this, but I think it means he's desperate now to tie up any loose ends. He's getting sloppy."

"According to TV that's when they start messing up and get caught."

"That's what I'm hoping, my sweet friend. That's what I am hoping."

The Drowning of Corinne Porter

Chapter Twenty-Three

"Not much gonna be left, eh?"

Oliver Tobias untied his tongue from the roof of his mouth and forced an answer for the young park ranger. "Nah." But maybe, since the fire had burned out so quickly, they'd get something. Anything they could go on.

The smoke had slowed from a roil to a wisp. He approached the front doorway. The door itself was gone, but the logs of the outer walls were so thick they barely even held a tinge of proof the fire had touched them. He placed a tentative foot over the threshold. It held solid.

The temperature inside the cabin was nearly unbearable, but no flames flickered anywhere he could see. In fact, other than the fact that the roof had crumbled and lay in random smoking heaps, the upstairs seemed relatively intact. Many of the

Mason jars had burst, their contents oozing down the shelves and onto the floor, giving the smoky aroma a tinge of burnt-soup scent. The table tilted at an odd angle, finding itself suddenly without the leg closest to the stairwell, and what was left of the wicker chair smoldered in a colorless gray pile.

He descended the stairs, but halfway down gave up and retreated. It was too hot and too smoky. As he broke into the fresh air outside, he drew a deep breath and an aching cough bent him double.

"You okay, man?" Blu asked, thumping him on the back a couple times.

"Yeah." He stood upright. "Yeah, I'll be fine."

"Wasn't too smart heading in there, if you ask me."

"I didn't."

"Righto. Well, the fire and forensics teams are on their way. Better let them handle it from here."

Oliver Tobias bit his tongue. Good thing he'd driven his own truck up here today and could leave anytime he wanted.

Annalise towel dried her hair as she walked to the front door to answer the incessant knocking.

She peered through the glass beside it and yanked it open. "What on earth, Zach?"

He rushed to embrace her. "I heard what happened at the cabin. Are you okay?"

She sank her head onto his chest and relished the feel of his arms around her. "I'm fine."

"You scared me."

"I promise. I'm fine."

"We need to talk."

Annalise pulled back. Moment over. "Yeah, I suppose we do, eh?"

"Can I come in?"

She held the door open wide for him. He smiled and made a beeline for the couch. He limped a little on the left and his arm didn't swing the same pendulum as the right, but other than that he seemed like himself. Annalise sighed. Good.

"Listen, Annalise, I owe you an apology. Or five."

She sat next to him. "Okay."

"You were right. I was taking my anger out on you. I shouldn't have ever done that. You've always been there for me." He grabbed her hand and looked her straight in the eye. "I know you had no choice but to act in the exact way you did. No, I do not blame you for my father's death. His actions led him down that road. I'm sorry I made you think I did."

"You remember what you said?"

"Not exactly, but it doesn't matter. I know I was wrong if I hurt you."

Annalise frowned.

"And if I ever do remember, I will apologize for exactly everything I said. Deal?"

"Do you still believe in me, Zach? That's the real issue. Do you still trust me?"

"Lise, of course I do. Since the sandbox."

She smiled.

"Do you think you can forgive me for being a total doofus?"

"I'll think about it." She flashed him a sideways look and a crooked grin.

"I'll take it. I love you."

"I love you too." And she knew she did. No matter what. But it may take a day or seventy to get past the hurt he'd caused. After all, she was still getting over the things her ex-husband had said, and she didn't even want a relationship with him anymore.

"Now, how can I help with the case?"

"You can't. No working. Kirk's orders."

"Okay. No working, but brainstorming over breakfast can't possibly be considered working."

She chuckled. "Breakfast?"

"Well, yeah. We need brain food to brainstorm."

"Of course we do."

"Whatcha got?"

"Nothing."

"Okay. Millie!"

Annalise's beagle raced in from down the hallway.

"We're going out. Hold down the fort." He rubbed the sweet dog's soft ears.

"We are, huh?"

"Cracker Barrel has missed me."

"Of course it has."

He tickled Annalise's sweat-pants-clad knee.

She jumped and giggled.

"Get dressed, lazy bones."

Seated at a four-top table in the front window, with the sunlight falling through the slightly warped glass, Annalise felt heavy. Relaxed for the first time in days. Her eyelids refusing to fully open, her lungs slowly inhaling the syrupy-coffee-tinged air. Her belly full of carbohydrates and bacon.

"Ready?"

"Hmm?"

"Ready to figure this thing out?"

She nodded.

"Tell me what you think comes next."

"The tie to UT could be the key to finding this guy."

"Who is he?"

She let her eyelids fall closed, crossed her arms over her chest, and leaned back into the chair. "He's a doctor or a nurse. He's quiet. Smart. The last man people in his life expect to be a serial killer. He has a wife and grown children. But he had a traumatic childhood. A mother who abused him repeatedly as a child. He never feels good enough. In fact, no matter how many successes he has, he hears his mother telling him he's worthless." Her eyes flew open.

"Wow. How much of that is from the profiler and how much from you?"

"About fifty-fifty. His victims are built like his mother, look like her somehow. He keeps them prisoner to assert his dominance. He rapes them to make himself feel like a man. He's never felt secure in that aspect."

"Why the university?"

"I don't know." She leaned onto her fist and stared at the candle dancing in the lamp on the table. Why the university? If he lives near the cabin somewhere—near enough to visit his victims when he wants—why drive to Knoxville, specifically to the campus, to kidnap his victims? She tapped her finger on her elbow. A muddy veil lifted. "He went to school there." Yes, that was it. He went to school there.

"Brilliant, Lise." Zach's smile beamed with pride. "What physical evidence do we have?"

"Not much. He's extremely careful. No hairs. No DNA. No fingerprints." She bit her lip. "The note."

"What note?"

"From John Prosise's house. Now that I know for sure the two are connected, maybe the note is connected too. I found it beside the fridge. Initials, I think, and a phone number."

"And put them all together…"

"We have something to search. Doctors with the initials LC in Knoxville and surrounding areas that went to school at UT."

"Bingo."

"He'll be scared right now. He knows we found his cabin. Or if he doesn't, he will soon when he comes back for Helene. What if we set a trap for him there?"

"It's worth a try."

"I'll call Kirk and Oliver Tobias."

"I'll research local docs."

Her mouth opened.

He raised his hands. "That's not working either. Working requires physical exertion."

She rolled her eyes. "Fine. But don't tell Kirk I gave you permission. That's your fight. Not mine. Come on."

Zach hated sitting at the house while Annalise was out there stalking a serial killer. It should be him at her side, not Oliver Tobias. He wasn't even a trained agent, for Pete's sake.

He jotted another name on the growing list. At least he was doing something useful instead of pacing.

Would one of these names lead them to their killer? He popped another peanut M&M in his mouth, a red one, and sent up a silent plea. Both for the team's safety and for the killer's arrest. And for his sanity until she returned safely to him.

Chapter Twenty-Four

Had they missed their chance already? Waited too long to "reset" the scene so it appeared normal? She'd hurried the plan through Kirk and then rounded up Oliver Tobias and a few men from KPD.

What if the killer had already come back, seen his cabin was destroyed and that Helene was gone, and fled, never to be seen again?

What if he smelled the smoke that clung to the air despite the passing hours and knew something was wrong?

What if they never caught him?

What if he went to a new city and started all over again?

What if he decided to finish Helene and Corinne off for good while they were out in the forest, their heads turned the wrong direction?

Annalise raised her hand in the prearranged signal, a loose thumbs up. Simple. Effective. The man to her left returned the signal and signaled the man to his left, until the sign made it all the way around the circle surrounding the killer's cabin.   When the man to her right flashed the thumb's up, she sighed. All was good. No sign of anyone.

She settled onto her backside, leaning against a tree trunk, crouching lower behind the dead log in front of her, and tried to still the trembling in her hands.

Late afternoon sunlight broke through the canopy in long, angled rays, touching the ground like flashlights brightening fragrant layers of pine needles and moss.

How many more of these lost little cabins sat out here? Someone should look into that and do an inventory to make sure nothing other than chipmunks and snakes occupied any others.

Sweat trickled down her back, soaked her elbow creases, and wetted the bends of her knees.

Sunset came without flourish. No brilliant reds and oranges. No clouds lit up like fluffy jewels. Just an unceremonious fade from sun to no sun. The leaves overhead created a black shield. Night insects began to chirrup and chorus in waves, but nothing else breathed life into the thick, inky night.

No more signals. No light. No noise. Just waiting. Interminable, indeterminate, ineffable night.

They'd missed him. He had already figured out they'd found his secret lair, and he wasn't coming back.

Annalise checked her faintly greenish-glowing watch. Nearly midnight. Time to wrap it up and go home. Plan something new. Try again.

A rustle of leaves down the hill behind her alerted her to a presence. It wasn't the leaves blowing in the wind overhead. After so many years loving the outdoors, she'd learned the way different footsteps sounded. The difference in weight, in number of legs, in gait. Each made a unique noise as they plodded through the leaf litter.

And this particular shuffling of feet was owned by a bipod, either sasquatch or a human being. Annalise didn't believe in fairy tales. She drew her gun and readied her flashlight, pointing it downhill and listening.

"Freeze!" She clicked the light on. It took a moment to spot anything other than thick, packed-together tree trunks. A thin figure moved at the fringe of her light, disappearing into the shadows. "I said freeze!"

In a matter of a few seconds, Oliver Tobias and the other men from their team arrived at her side.

"There!" She pointed down the hill. "Someone was there."

Ten flashlights shone into the dark night, and their heavy footsteps thudded through the leaves, drowning out any chance of hearing the fleeing suspect.

Annalise froze and held up her hand. "Everyone stop!"

The men scattered throughout the forest came to a quick halt.

"Listen." She tilted her head and squeezed her eyes shut. She was met with silence. So pure and full it made her heart stop.

Whoever had been there was gone.

Chapter Twenty-Five

"Oliver, it's good to see you."

Corinne's radiant smile squelched any thought of correcting her he may have had. Besides, those three syllables sounded just right coming from those pink-tinged, full lips. He had been staring.

She blushed. "How are you today?"

"Good." He cleared his throat. Where had that froggy-cricket squeak come from? "How are you holding up?"

"I'm great. Heading home later today."

His heart sank. Home. Far away from him.

"You'll come see me, won't you?"

From the bottom of the Grand Canyon to soaring in the clouds, his heart leapt. He managed an awkward nod. What was wrong with him? Sheesh. He'd been through four deployments, seen men in all stages of life and death, nearly been killed so many times he'd need more fingers and toes to count them all, and dealt with stress unimaginable to most civilians. But this girl—this girl—had him quaking in his own skin.

And it felt wonderful.

Like life being resuscitated in his veins, encouraged back to breathing by her smile. He wanted to fill every cell with the essence of her.

"Oliver Tobias, you're staring again."

The blush that crept into his face actually hurt his cheeks. He couldn't meet her gaze.

"Thank you for coming to see me again. I rather enjoy your company, you know."

She did? Why? His company was nothing to brag about. No eloquent speech, no anything special. "Thank you, ma'am."

She giggled. "Oh, don't you dare ma'am me, sir."

His gaze whipped to hers.

"We have been through something monumental here. Have we not?"

He nodded.

"Far too intimate for formalities like ma'am and sir." She reached for his hand.

He gave it without even thinking. And when she touched him, his skin tingled to life.

"We're friends. Forever."

And he'd go to the ends of the earth for her friendship. Forever. Finding words impossible, he swallowed.

"I like your tattoo." She pointed with her free hand to his biceps.

"Thanks."

"A memorial of your military career, no doubt."

"Yes."

Her gaze clouded over with sadness. "I think I will get a tattoo too. Something that reminds me of my rescue, instead of this garish mark."

He'd nearly forgotten their serial killer had marred her flawless, creamy skin. A flash of heat burst through him.

"Something that reminds me of you."

"Me?"

"It will be much happier for me than what it currently reminds me of."

"I'm honored."

She smiled, though the faraway look in her eyes didn't leave.

"I need to go." When would he see her again?

As if reading his mind, she grabbed a pen and paper from the desk next to her hospital bed. "Here. You call me. Soon."

"I will." He wouldn't dare miss that invitation. Not for anything in the world.

Zach handed Annalise the list of doctors he'd compiled. "It's long. Way longer than I'd have thought." He glanced at Oliver Tobias seated across the counter in Annalise's kitchen. He liked the guy, whether he wanted to admit it or not.

Annalise flipped through the notebook pages. "Wow. It is a lot."

"I've only looked for doctors in a fifty-mile radius of Knoxville with the initials LC. I've then highlighted the ones who graduated from UT. I can't believe how many there are."

"Me either." She sighed.

"Can I see?"

Zach passed the list to Oliver Tobias.

"Only one way to start."

"How's that?" Annalise asked.

"One at a time."

Zach chuckled. "He isn't wrong, Lise."

"Alphabetically or by radius to our location?" She was half-joking, but the guys were right. They had to start somewhere.

"Radius. Man, I wish I could come with you." Zach hated her leaving him behind. Hated how vulnerable it made him feel to have her out there without him. "You'll watch her back, right?"

Oliver Tobias nodded. "Like a hawk."

Annalise's phone jingled. "Hi, Kirk. What's up?"

Zach studied her face as she listened. It paled, and her eyes grew wide. She hung up only a minute later. "What is it?"

"There's been another abduction."

Zach's stomach dropped. By the look on his face, Oliver Tobias felt something similar. Defeat hung heavy in the air. He placed his hand on Annalise's shoulder. "We're gonna get him."

"What if—"

"Don't go there, Lise. We'll get him. In time to save her too."

"He's getting scared. Moving faster. And his cabin is out of the question as a hiding spot." Oliver Tobias rose to his feet. "That means he's had to scramble for a new place to keep his victim. Less secure. Easier to find."

"I hope so."

Zach could feel the renewed tension in her shoulder as she replied. "Come on. Let's get started."

Annalise stood. "Radius from the cabin. Rather than radius from here." She retrieved her binder of hiking maps from the shelf between the dining area and living room, the one she kept updated and handy for times just like these, he knew.

She removed a map from a plastic sleeve protector and unfolded it. After studying it for a moment, she pointed. "Here. We start here. How many docs are there in Wears Valley/Townsend?"

Zach checked the list. "Fourteen. But only three that graduated from or attended UT at some point."

"All right. Let's go." Oliver Tobias moved toward the front door. "I'll give you guys a moment." He disappeared outside.

"You'll be our home base?"

Zach nodded. "I want to come with you."

"I want you to too. But more than that, I want you safe. And healing. And not breaking that brain of yours again."

"But—"

"No buts. You need every brain cell you have left."

"Hardy har." He wrapped his arms around her. *Thank you, Lord, that she's letting me hold her again without bristling like a porcupine.* "I'll be your home base. Check in after every single stop. Please."

"Will do."

He kissed her forehead before she had a chance to pull away. "I love you."

"I love you too."

"Be careful."

"Of course. Oliver Tobias is a good partner."

"Not as good as me, I hope."

She smiled up at him. "I'll see you soon. Keep your phone handy."

"Deal." He smiled, but inside he didn't feel it.

They arrived on the University of Tennessee graduates' doorsteps and pounded with the urgency they felt but couldn't express. Annalise took the lead, flashing the photos of the victims and asking if they had been seen recently. It was such a long shot, it wasn't even a shot.

"Mrs. Carson, has your husband been acting strangely lately?"

At stop number two, "Has Dr. Cooper been missing at odd hours?"

Did any of their bosses have secret cabins in the Smokies where they tortured and murdered women?

It didn't take long for Annalise to realize their tactics were pointless. No one wanted to answer questions.

At the fourth door, she knocked with a lighter hand and waited. She should just leave. Head back to the office and start all over again for the umpteenth time. But there was a young woman out there somewhere who needed their help.

A woman with barely-there wrinkles and dark hair streaked with a few stray silvers answered the door. "Yes?"

"Are you Mrs. Clark?

"Yes. May I help you?"

"I'm Special Agent Annalise Baker. I'm investigating the disappearance of several local women. We are canvassing some of the local neighborhoods and hoping to find a witness with information. May I come in?"

"I'm not sure…"

"It will only take a minute, ma'am. Please."

"Oh, I suppose." Mrs. Clark opened the door and motioned Annalise and Oliver Tobias inside.

"I have some photos here. If you could look at them and see if you recognize any of the young women, it would be helpful."

Mrs. Clark rubbed the back of her neck. "Okay. Um, yes."

Annalise pulled her phone from her pocket and held the first image up for Mrs. Clark.

She shook her head.

Annalise quickly scrolled through the remaining photos, ending with their newest missing woman, Kira Lee.

On the last one, Mrs. Clark's hand stopped moving against her neck. Briefly. But it stopped nonetheless.

"Do you recognize her?"

"No. No, I don't recognize any of these women." She drew a deep breath and straightened her shirt. "What exactly happened to them?"

"Three of them are dead. Two of them were abducted and rescued but may never be the same. One is missing as of yesterday evening."

Mrs. Clark covered her mouth. "Awful. Simply awful."

"Running on the assumption the same serial killer kidnapped her, our latest victim is running out of time. Fast."

Mrs. Clark stared over Annalise's shoulder.

Annalise spun to find a balding, thin man in the doorway. "Dr. Clark?"

"I am. Ruthie, did you invite them in?"

Mrs. Clark nodded. "They're looking for some missing women, dear. Asking people for help."

He stepped to his wife's side and put a protective arm around her shoulder. "I'm sorry, as I'm sure my wife has told you, we haven't seen anything suspicious."

"Of course. We knew it was not likely we'd get any information, but truth is we're growing more and more desperate by the day."

"Such a sad situation, Leon. Isn't it? All those young lives snuffed out so early?"

Dr. Clark nodded. "Sorry we can't be of more help."

Annalise handed him a business card. "If you think of anything, please call."

He nodded.

She started to turn but stopped and flashed the photo of Kira Lee once more. "Have you seen this woman?"

Dr. Clark didn't look at the photo. "No."

Outside, with the door closed behind them, Oliver Tobias leaned in. "You're sneaky as a tunnel rat."

"I have no idea what you mean."

"I've watched you with all these doctors' wives and now Dr. Clark. You know there's no chance they've seen the victims unless they are the killer. These women don't live anywhere nearby and weren't abducted here."

She smiled.

"You're hoping one of them will slip up and show you something they don't mean to reveal in their body language or facial expression, aren't you?"

"Precisely." She paused. "Did you notice the shed out back, Oliver Tobias?"

He nodded as he slid into the passenger seat of her SUV. "Seemed pretty standard operating procedure for this neighborhood. Quaint, white homes with shutters and gardens."

"I agree. But the padlock on the front was dangling. Odd, don't you think?"

"Not sure. Could be. Could also be we're being overly antsy at the moment. I've seen it happen a million times. You know something needs to break or happen and you start imagining it is in the smallest of details."

"Yeah, maybe." She buckled her seatbelt. "Okay, four down, ten to go." She checked in with Zach and headed for the next house. Each of the remaining stops were so similar to the first four, she could've scripted them, except for the fact that Dr. Clark had been home. But she couldn't exactly fault a doctor for taking a day off. Especially not a plastic surgeon on a Friday afternoon.

Chapter Twenty-Six

"It's a dead end, Kirk." Annalise crossed her arms over her chest and sank into the chair on the opposite side of his desk from him.

"Well, it was a good try."

"I knew it was a shot in the dark, but I'd really hoped it would work."

"I know. Me too. Questioning these guys was a reasonable way to approach it. Unfortunately, this killer is incredibly intelligent and probably saw through it, if we did happen to speak with him."

A shiver ran down her spine. Had they been face to face with their murderer? Would she have gotten some vibe from him, if so? "Have you gotten the ME's report for the new bodies we found?"

Sara L. Foust

Kirk's lips pressed into a thin line before he handed her a folder.

Her going behind his back on the dog search still hung awkwardly between them. She flipped through the files. Victims strangulated. Same marking on the hip. Same drugs in their system. Same physical abuse. Same lack of forensic evidence that could be used to tie victims to killer. "It's definitely him."

Kirk nodded. "What do you want to do next?"

Annalise shrugged. "The marking—I thought it would help. I can't even figure out what it means. Another dead end." She hung her head.

"What's next, Annalise? Keep going."

She drew in a slow, deep breath and blew it out through pursed lips. "UT campus is a big place. It's half of downtown Knoxville. But it's the next best lead we've got."

Kirk nodded. "Have you looked at where each victim was abducted and plotted it on the map?"

"We don't know where the deceased ones were taken."

"True, but how are they each connected to UT?"

"One was a student. One worked at the Starbucks in the main student's hall. One was janitorial services in the English building. Of course, everything is slower right now since it's summer term. There aren't as many students on campus."

"Might be why he is striking now. Fewer witnesses?"

"Good possibility."

"And Corinne and Helene?"

"Helene isn't connected through UT. I believe he took her because of the news story."

"Right."

He was stream of consciousnessing—that wasn't a word—her. Trying to get her to stop focusing so narrowly and just let the information flow fluidly. She sighed. "Corinne worked in the library and was walking home to her apartment near the Old City. The newest victim was last seen leaving Burger King on the strip. She was headed back to her near-campus apartment."

"What's the central region where they're connected? Is there one?"

She pressed her eyelids closed. "I need a map." When she opened them, he'd produced one. It lay flat on his desk. "Thanks."

He handed her a stack of mini-sticky tabs.

She placed the colored papers on each of the women's known working or housing locations. "They're all near the stadium."

"Why?"

She tilted her head as she pictured that part of campus. "It's a main artery. Quick access to Alcoa Highway." She pressed her lips together. "And to the mountains."

"Good." He tapped a pencil on the desktop. "Some of it is assumption, but it is logical.

Sara L. Foust

Gather a team. Get people in cars on stakeouts. Tonight."

"Yes, sir." She rose to leave.

"Oh, and Annalise."

"Yes."

"Good work."

"I didn't get him, Kirk."

"No, but you saved Helene and you did it without going behind my back. This is the agent I've been missing—we've all been missing."

She blushed. "Thank you."

Motioning for Oliver Tobias to follow her from his lobby post, she exited into the garden and began pacing. Mind racing. Heart skipping beats. Was this their last hope? Their last put-all-the-eggs-in-one-basket chance?

"Talk to me, Annalise."

"We need a team, and we need it fifteen minutes ago. We need to look at the most logical places on campus where our killer would be prowling."

"But he's already got a victim. We think. Would he be looking for another?"

She stopped in her tracks. "Good question." She whipped out her phone and dialed Kirk's profiler friend.

Jackie's cheerful voice came on the line.

"This is Agent Baker, from SMIF. We need some help."

"Sure. What's up?"

Annalise filled her in about the current status of the case.

"Oh, yeah. He's gonna be as nervous as a possum up a tree with a dog barking at its base."

Annalise grinned. Interesting phrasing.

"He is spiraling. His secret hideout is wrecked. You've saved two victims. There's no way this guy's not panicking right now."

"Do you think it's possible our latest abductee is still alive?"

"No. Not likely. He's going to be rapidly accelerating and spinning out of control. He'll strike again within twenty-four hours, I'd almost bet on it."

Annalise's heart ached for Kira. Though they had no definitive proof their serial killer had taken this newest missing woman, Annalise knew. She just knew it was him. "Wow. Are you sure?"

"Not as sure as betting on the Derby winner beefed up on steroids, but yeah, sure as it'll rain in spring."

"Thank you."

"If you're going to catch him, now's the time. He's going to be more careless. More desperate to prove his point, to fulfill the need he has to be dominant over these women. But he's also going to be more dangerous. He'll be feeling cornered as a bear in a trap with a belly full of drug-laced doughnuts. Keep that in mind."

She thanked Jackie and hung up, then she turned to Oliver Tobias. "If we can't find him now—"

"We will."

"She may already be dead."

"I heard."

Kirk burst out the door. "Annalise, we've got her."

"What?"

"Kira Lee. She was dropped in front of the Fort Sanders ER."

Annalise wrinkled her brow. "When?"

"Early this morning."

Her heart flew into a gallop. Why had it taken them so long to call them? Was Kira okay? How had she gotten there?

"Annalise." Oliver Tobias stared at her.

She tilted her head.

"Well, come on." He smiled. "Let's go."

"Right. Yeah." She jostled herself into motion.

Chapter Twenty-Seven

Annalise skidded to a stop at the nurse's desk. "Kira Lee?"

The nurse frowned.

Annalise flashed her badge. "It's urgent we speak with her."

"You'll have to speak with him."

Annalise turned in the direction she'd pointed. A tall, The Rock-sized policeman stood down a short hallway. She drew a deep breath. "Wait here, Oliver Tobias."

He nodded.

She approached the officer with a smile, showed him her badge and assumed a casual stance. "Sir, we are investigating a case involving missing women and several murders in Sevier County. We believe Kira Lee was abducted by the same man."

The officer crossed his arms over his chest, grasping biceps that looked more like thighs.

She swallowed. "Please, it's imperative we speak with her."

"Ms. Lee has been through a lot. She's not taking visitors, and unless you have proof she's involved with your case, it will have to wait."

"She has marks on her wrists and ankles where she's been bound."

His white-knuckled grip loosened.

"And a strange mark on her lower back or hip that looks like a burn."

"How did you—"

"She's been drugged and assaulted and never saw his face."

His arms dropped to his sides. Tears sprang to his eyes. "She's my sister."

Her stomach clenched. "I am so sorry. I can't imagine how you must feel. But I want to catch this guy, and she may be our best hope. Please, may I speak with her?"

He dipped his chin a fraction.

"Thank you." Annalise slipped into the room. "Ms. Lee?"

A beautiful, dark-haired young woman turned haunted eyes on Annalise.

"I'm Special Agent Baker. May I ask you some questions?"

Kira continued to stare through Annalise. She slowly approached the bed and slid a chair close.

"I know you've been through a nightmare. I'm sorry to bother you."

Kira's eyes shimmered with unshed tears.

"How did you get here?"

She turned her head and swallowed hard.

"It's okay. Take your time."

The clock on the wall ticked loud seconds off as Annalise waited and held her breath.

"She brought me." Kira's voice was barely above a whisper.

"She who?"

"His wife, I think."

"Do you know her name?"

"Ruth. She said her name was Ruth."

Annalise bit back an excited yelp. "Thank you." On her way out, she patted Kira's brother's shoulder and nodded. Then she sprinted to where Oliver Tobias waited and whispered, "We've got him."

His eyebrows lifted.

"Come on."

She called Kirk. "We need backup."

"You've got a lead?"

"We've got the killer, Kirk."

"Okay. Run with it, Annalise. Whatever you need."

She gave him the address.

"I'll meet you there. You'll be running point."

"Deal." Her next call was to her friends at the KPD. She drove as fast as she could hang the curves safely and pulled into the cul-de-sac near

Dr. Clark's home just behind the police team and Kirk.

The men and women gathered in a semi-circle around Annalise. She showed them pictures of Dr. Clark and Ruth. "Keep in mind, the wife is innocent. And he will be unpredictable. Dangerous. Think coyote with one foot in a trap."

Annalise led the team up a side street and motioned for them to encircle the doctor's house. At her nod, they moved in as one unit—a noose tightening with each forward step around Leon's property.

She tiptoed onto the porch and peeked through the beveled glass. The afternoon sunlight cast kaleidoscope shapes onto the hardwood. "Anyone see anything?" she whispered into the mic on her shoulder.

A hushed reply crackled back. "Got something. Someone's down. Looks unconscious."

"Go! Everyone in!"

Annalise burst through the front door, with Oliver Tobias on her heel and Kirk right behind him. "Dr. Leon Clark!"

There was no response.

She rounded the corner, around the stairwell and into the den. Her feet froze. An officer stooped over Mrs. Clark, lying in a heap on the floor. Another stood watch over them both. Her heart fluttered as she knelt. "Is she—"

"No. She has a pulse," the officer replied.

Annalise rolled Mrs. Clark onto her back and gasped. Blood streaked a path down her cheek and bruises had begun to grow purple around her eyes. "Ruth?"

The older woman's swollen eyelids fluttered.

"We're going to get you some help." She looked up. "Call for an ambulance."

"I've... never... seen... him—"

"Shh, it's okay, Mrs. Clark."

"He hit me."

Boulders sank in Annalise's gut. "I can see that. Do you know where he went?"

Ruth shook her head and winced. "Is she... okay?"

"She will be. Eventually."

A tear trickled down Mrs. Clark's cheek. "I can't believe I didn't—" She stifled a sob.

Annalise squeezed Ruth's hand. What could she possibly say?

As soon as the ambulance left with Ruth, Annalise joined the men in the garage out back. If it wasn't for the bed in the center of the room, it would be an ordinary man's garage. The ties at the head and foot of the bed turned Annalise's stomach. This man had to be stopped. Where would he go? Somewhere he felt safe.

He couldn't go to the cabin.

He couldn't come back here.

Work? UT campus?

"Agent Baker?" An officer approached her.

"Yes?"

"Found a system rigged up to the bed. It was pressure sensored under the mattress. Any change in weight was meant to trip a system that let gas leak into the room and that would've triggered an ignition spark. The whole place could've gone up, 'cept the line connected to the bed was too loose to pull the plug in the piping."

That explained the cabin. "He must've been in a hurry." Thank goodness. Kira and Ruthie were both alive because of the "good" doctor's rush. "Thanks."

The officer nodded and stepped away. She turned. "Come on, Oliver Tobias. Guys, you got this covered?"

Kirk nodded as Oliver Tobias approached her.

Dr. Clark's office parking lot was empty, save two cars. Annalise pounded on the locked front door until a woman with raised eyebrows and a frown answered. "Dr. Clark? Where is he?"

She stood with the door partially opened, balanced against her hip. "He left early today."

"What was he driving?"

"The van."

"What van? What does it look like?"

The woman crossed her arms over her chest. "The blue one. He sometimes picks up oxygen tanks himself. Knows the refill guy or something like that. Why? Has something happened to Dr. Clark?"

Annalise met the woman's gaze and held it a fraction longer than necessary. "If Dr. Clark returns, you dial 9-1-1 immediately. Do you understand me?"

The woman nodded.

"He's dangerous." She placed her hand on the woman's arm. "I mean it."

Her face paled. "I don't understand."

"No time to explain. Do you know the license plate number?"

She nodded. "It's written in the office for the transport form. Stay here. I'll grab it." A few minutes later, she returned with a sheet of paper and handed it to Annalise.

"Thanks. Lock the doors. Get home if you can."

Annalise hopped in the truck with Oliver Tobias and called in the APB on the van. "Every available officer needs to be on campus looking for this man." The scene at the cabin replayed in her mind. On its heels, the bruises on Ruth's face. "Approach cautiously. Consider him highly dangerous. But he should not be allowed to escape, under any circumstances."

Chapter Twenty-Eight

Night settled in as Oliver Tobias tapped his finger on his thigh. One finger. That's all that allowed an outsider a clue about the impatient anxiety roiling through him.

Annalise fidgeted, spoke about nothing frequently, and chewed gum, piece after piece. Even if he didn't know her, he'd be able to pick up on her angst. "Where is he?"

"Could be anywhere 'bout now."

"Not what I wanted to hear."

"Same answer I gave you last time you asked."

"Still not what I want to hear." She grinned. "But at least you're still answering."

In five more minutes, the team would radio in, one by one giving a sit. rep. Annalise would get her hopes up yet again and be even more frustrated than she was currently.

He knew. It'd been going on for six hours now. Her SUV smelled like stale coffee and tacos, and the nontraditional, quick dinner they'd eaten a couple hours ago was long gone—all but the odor.

Annalise's phone dinged yet again.

"Zach?"

She nodded.

"Every fifteen minutes, like clockwork." For six hours. Whether from the cramped vehicle with its unpleasant aroma or the fact that he couldn't stop thinking about Corinne, Annalise's phone sounds and constant twitching were about to drive him nuts. Could be the fact it was after midnight and he missed the quiet mountain too. It felt good to be part of something like this again, he wasn't gonna lie. But it kept him off-kilter, and that was unacceptable.

"What are you over there brooding about, Oliver Tobias?"

"Brooding?" Like a hen? "I am not brooding."

"Look, I know this has been different for you. But I want you to know how much I appreciate you. I wouldn't have gotten to this point without your help."

Negativity flowed from him. His shoulders relaxed. "You're welcome, Annalise. I'm glad to help stop this monster."

She smiled.

"But I will be glad to get back to the mountain when it's over."

"You don't think you'd consider a career with us?"

He blinked. "Career?"

"You haven't thought of it?"

"To be honest, no. I haven't the same training as you all. I'm not sure I'm a good fit."

"You're a good fit. Especially with a recommendation from a current officer."

He lifted his eyebrow.

"You'd make a great agent, Oliver Tobias. Please think about it."

"What about Kirk?"

"I think he'd agree with me, but of course we could discuss it. If it's something you're interested in."

Was he? "I'll think about it." He glanced out the front window, staring into the lamplit street silently waiting out the long night under the yellow glow. "Annalise?"

"Yeah?"

"Look."

In slow motion, Annalise turned her head and recognition dawned, like a wet fuse. A dark blue van had turned into the street ahead and pulled to the curb. The tendril of white exhaust curled lazily from its tailpipe for a moment and then stopped. The license plate matched.

"Oh my, Oliver Tobias. That's him."

They flung open their doors at the same time.

"Slowly," she whispered to him as they rounded the front of the SUV.

Dr. Clark emerged from the van, glanced around, and immediately spotted them. Even in the low light, Annalise could see the color drain from his face. He backed a few stumbling paces and then broke into a sprint down the sidewalk.

She and Oliver Tobias burst into a run. Oliver Tobias passed her up like she was standing still and turned the corner ahead, following Dr. Clark. She radioed the team with their location. "We've got him! Come quick!"

Sliding around the corner slowly, she spotted Oliver Tobias ahead, motionless, his weapon drawn.

"Where'd he go?"

"I don't know. It's like he just vanished."

Annalise bristled. Something wasn't right. Movement to her right drew her attention. A cold, hard object pressed against her temple.

"Don't move."

She couldn't think over the sound of the blood whooshing against her eardrums with each rapid beat.

Oliver Tobias took a step closer.

The gun against her head pressed tighter, sending shards of pain cascading down her spine.

"Don't move!"

Oliver Tobias froze.

"Toss your gun in the dumpster."

Oliver Tobias hesitated for a moment and then did as instructed.

Dr. Clark sighed. "You are smarter than I gave you credit for."

Finally, she found her tongue. "Is that supposed to be a compliment?"

"Take it as you like." He buried his nose in Annalise's hair and inhaled deeply as he removed her weapon from her hand and tucked it in his belt.

Nausea crept up her throat. "There's not a single thing I like about you, Dr. Clark. Not. One."

He chuckled. "Maybe you aren't. Insulting the man holding a gun to your brain isn't brilliant. Ah well. What shall we do with you now, eh?" Grabbing a handful of her hair, he pulled her backward with him as he exited the alleyway.

Her scalp screamed and her leaden legs grew heavier with each step. Help! Had she said it out loud? With her pulse beating against her veins and a clammy sweat coating her hands, she fought against Dr. Clark's iron grip.

Oliver Tobias took a few steps her direction.

Dr. Clark fired off two quick shots. One bounced gravel and chunks of asphalt against Oliver Tobias's lower legs. The second found a mark. Oliver Tobias let out a quick moan and dove behind the same dumpster.

"No!" Annalise couldn't tell exactly where he'd been hit, but she'd guess abdomen. "Oliver Tobias!"

Dr. Clark tightened his grip. "Shut up."

Oliver Tobias was hit. She had to help him! Had to save—

A sharp, heavy blow to the nape of her neck left her breathless.

Dr. Clark dragged her around the corner of the building and into the empty street.

"No, no, no, no!" Was she screaming aloud? This couldn't be happening. If he got her to his van, what then? Where was their backup? How was this skinny man so strong?

He released her hair and wrapped his arm around her neck. "Stop fighting, dear. It's really so much easier if you just give in."

Fuzzy edges narrowed in on her peripheral vision. Her body grew heavier.

Zach! Where are you? No, Oliver Tobias. Or Zach?

Zach held his breath to keep from screaming. He waited in the dark, his gun drawn, his eyes struggling for details. Just a little closer. Then he could get that man's grubby fingers off Annalise.

Just a step or two more.

Pitiful moans escaped her. She sounded desperate. Frantic. His heart pulled out of his chest and flew to her. But he couldn't move. Not yet. The timing had to be perfect.

He wasn't supposed to be here. Wasn't supposed to be involved. But thank goodness he didn't always do what he was supposed to.

Moments ago, when Annalise and Oliver Tobias had jumped from the SUV, he'd exited his vehicle parked farther down the street, hidden in the shadow of a box truck.

He hadn't made it to the corner before this man had backed into his line of sight, dragging Annalise with him, and every cell in his body had zinged back to life.

Crouched behind the man's van, Zach's grip on his handgun tightened. Sirens echoed from several directions, flying through the otherwise quiet Knoxville night.

He peeked out and darted back in. They were almost there, but Annalise had gone completely limp. He swallowed the lump in his throat.

When the suspect threw open the side door, Zach sprang. "Freeze!"

The suspect dropped Annalise. She fell halfway into the van, her legs at awkward angles on the sidewalk. The man spun.

Zach pulled his trigger.

The suspect dropped like a fifty-pound sack of feed. Instantly. While the bounce of the gunshot echoed off the buildings and stung Zach's ears.

"Zach?" Oliver Tobias's voice rang out.

"Yeah, man. I'm good."

"What're you doing here? How did you—"

Zach flashed him a brief smile, as Oliver Tobias trotted towards him. "I'm stubborn as a mule. You okay?" Blood seeped through Oliver Tobias's fingers pressed to his side.

"I'll manage."

"Ambulance?"

Oliver Tobias shook his head. "I'll get stitches after I know she's okay."

Zach stepped over the dead suspect and swooped Annalise into his arms. "Lise?"

Her eyelids fluttered.

"Lise, wake up." He brushed her bangs aside and planted a kiss against her forehead. "Love, come on now. Wake up."

Her eyes popped open, panic swimming in the dilated pupils. "Zach?"

"In the flesh."

"Where is he?" She struggled to free herself from his embrace.

"He's dead, Lise. Relax. Take a few breaths."

Her hand flew to her throat and rubbed. "Breathing is good."

He smiled. "I am the only one allowed to take your breath away from now on. Deal?"

She tilted her head sideways. "Deal."

Epilogue

Three months later…

"It's amazing, Oliver Tobias." Annalise hugged him. "It suits you."

He blushed as he pulled out the deck chair for her. "Thanks."

"How's your side?"

"Right as rain on a summer afternoon."

Annalise chuckled. "I'm glad that awful, evil man had such bad aim."

"As am I. It would stink to survive two deployments in an actual war zone and be taken out in an alleyway in Knoxville by a crazy old man."

"So true." She squeezed his arm and then sat and took in the view. Oliver Tobias's new home was breathtaking. Nestled at the base of a sky-kissing mountain, the deck he'd added to the south of his yurt fit perfectly with the essence of the place.

Zach took the seat to her left and smiled at her. "It's perfect here, isn't it?"

She nodded.

Corinne sat to her right and grinned at Oliver Tobias, who took the last seat at the four-top. In the middle of the table, next to the flickering candle, cheeseburgers and mounds of corn and French fries awaited them.

"Oliver Tobias, thank you for the invite." Annalise patted her stomach. "I'm starving."

"Me too." Zach grinned.

"Aren't you always?" Oliver Tobias teased.

"And it's about time we did this double date we've been talking about for months now." Corinne grasped Oliver Tobias's hand.

The couple had fallen faster than stars. Annalise sighed. Falling in love. Falling into place.

The case was still fresh, but it was starting to fade into the recesses. Evenings like these, surrounded by her friends and with Zach at her side, made it easier to let go of the trauma of her first serial killer. The trauma of the mistakes she'd made, the death of Zach's father. The divorce. Everything. Made it easier to march forward. Made it easier to let go. Like the leaves starting to turn that would soon float to the ground, she could release the pain. A little at a time. And let it fly away into the blurry lines of the past.

THE END

Dear Readers,

I hope you have enjoyed continuing Annalise and Zach's story.

Check out the final book in the Smoky Mountain Suspense Series, number four, *The Bludgeoning of Kirk Johnson*, which is available for preorder on Amazon now. Coming November 2022.

Murder reaches too close to home this time...

When Smoky Mountain Investigative Force's lead agent, Kirk Johnson, is slain, Special Agents Annalise Baker and Zachary Leebow are forced to face and solve a crime they never anticipated...

...With an outcome no one sees coming.

Pssst... Just a quick reminder, if you haven't already, please join my newsletter. I'd love to have you! Sign up now and get my free eBook novella, *Of Walls*, delivered right to your inbox. Plus get the inside scoop on all my new releases and giveaways and receive newsletters where we can connect, get to know each other, and pray for one another. Here is the link (or click on the image below): http://eepurl.com/cfqP5H

Acknowledgments

I am blessed to be constantly surrounded by people who love me, support me, and push me to be better. Thank you—all of you. I wouldn't have made it without each of you in my life.

Thank you, Ron, for brainstorming and creating Oliver Tobias with me and listening while I go on and on about fictional people and crimes as if they are real. I am beyond thankful that you are you.

Thank you, Becky, for your extremely valuable feedback. My books wouldn't be the same without your help!

About the Author

Sara is a multi-published, award-winning author, freelance editor, owner of Silver Lining Literary Services, LLC, and mother of five who writes surrounded by the beauty of East Tennessee. She earned her bachelor's degree in Animal Science from the University of Tennessee and is a member of American Christian Fiction Writers, The Christian PEN, and Sigma Tau Delta English Honor Society. Sara finds inspiration in her faith, her family, and the beauty of nature. When she isn't writing, you can find her reading, camping, and spending time outdoors. To learn more about her and her work or to become a part of her email friend's group, please visit www.saralfoust.com.